Writers of the Mendocino Coast

At the Edge

Anthology 2013

At The Edge

WRITERS OF THE MENDOCINO COAST, ANTHOLOGY 2013
Edited by Norma Watkins
Copyright © 2013 by Gray Whale Press

No part of this book may be reproduced or transmitted in any form or by any means now known or to be invented, electronically or mechanically, including photocopying, recording, or by any information storage and retrieval system without written permission from the publisher, except for the inclusion of brief quotations in a review.

For information, or to order additional copies of this book, contact:
Gray Whale Press
P. O. Box 762, Fort Bragg, CA 95437
www.writersmendocinocoast.org

Cover design by Doug Fortier
Interior design by Janet Ashford
Cover art, "Sailing to Byzantium" by Alena Guest, www.alenaguest.com
Back cover photograph by Patty Joslyn
Interior photographs by Janet Ashford

ISBN: 978-0-9886091-0-5 print
 978-0-9886091-1-2 ebook

Contents

Non-fiction	**The Way Out**	Ginny Rorby	1
Fiction	**Nightwriting**	Alena Deerwater	9
Fiction	**The Rescue 1909**	Lea Callan	16
Non-fiction	**Secrets**	Fran Schwartz	25
Fiction	**Moby Jane, Princess of Whales**	Holly Tannen	30
Non-fiction	**Finding Myself in York**	Neal Metcalf	37
Poetry	**In This Place**	Jewels Marcus	47
Fiction	**Hush**	Gloria Jorgensen	48
Non-fiction	**Excerpt from Standing in Gorda**	Tony Camarda	57
Non-fiction	**Rip Van Winkle and Me**	Aron Lee Bowe	65
Fiction	**Folie Beaujon**	Molly Dwyer	69
Non-fiction	**Piano, Piano**	Nona Smith	78
Fiction	**Blue Waves**	Patty Joslyn	84
Non-fiction	**Queen of Cuts**	Kathleen Damiani	86
Poetry	**Flying Instructions**	Cheri Ause	94
Fiction	**Suspended Animation**	Jan Edwards	96
Non-fiction	**24 Hours**	Lew Mermelstein	103
Non-fiction	**Mother's Ire**	Marylyn Scott	109
Fiction	**Outlaw Ford**	Malcolm Macdonald	114
Poetry	**The Next Coming**	Jewels Marcus	122
Non-fiction	**War Babies**	Willow Arthur	124
Fiction	**On the Thursday Before Easter**	Norma Watkins	131
Non-fiction	**Anthracite**	Charles Furey	138
Non-fiction	**Donald from the Hame**	Janet Ashford	141
	Acknowledgments		150
	About the Authors		151

Praise for *At the Edge*

At the Edge is an impressive collection, beautifully put together. The writing is by turns funny, revealing, surprising, and heartbreaking, andit's consistently just plain good."
—Christie Olson Day, owner of Gallery Bookshop, Mendocino

In these writings—heartfelt, unrestrained, eagerly told—you can feel the richness of an entire community, the goodness of it, how deep and powerfully the emotions run. The openness and honesty with which these stories and essays are written makes them each feel like little, individual gifts.
—Josh Weil, author of *The New Valley: Novellas* (Grove Press, 2009)

At the edge of control is where the good stories are. The Writers of the Mendocino Coast tackle what it means to be up against the knife's edge or the cliff's ledge, forced to fight, dig, swim, or fast talk your way to safer ground. Photographs of the area's rugged coastline by Janet Ashford mirror the salty character and turbulent beauty of these well-crafted stories, essays and poems.
—Susan Bono, editor, *Tiny Lights: A Journal of Personal Narrative*

A wonderful medley of voices, each rising to its own unique note."
—Shirin Bridges, head goose at Goosebottom Books, author of *The Thinking Girl's Treasury of Dastardly Dames* series

They say all the wild people move to the edge of the continent; after reading this anthology, I'm convinced it's true.
—Jody Gehrman, playwright and author of the *Triple Shot Betty* novels

Editor's Note

WHEN WE DECIDED on a theme for our first anthology, At the Edge, seemed a natural. We are on the western edge of our continent and the Pacific Ocean bashes against the cliffs. The stories selected for this first volume are about living at that edge, but expand metaphorically—from a newborn sliding from a railway handcar, to a death off those cliffs. But there is more than meets the eye to a writing life here on the edge. We live where three tectonic plates meet. They bump and grind against each other, causing the land to shudder, crack, and splinter. The events in our lives, and in the stories we tell, reflect the movement beneath our feet.
—Norma Watkins, Editor

President's Message

WE'RE A SMALL COMMUNITY filled with enormous talent. In an area with fewer than 20,000 people, our writing club has a membership of 70. This first volume contains the best of the members' work from 2012. If you write or enjoy good writing, please join us.
—Doug Fortier, President of the Writers of the Mendocino Coast, www.writersmendocinocoast.org

"Greenwood Beach," Janet Ashford

ABOUT THE AUTHORS

Willow Arthur is a metaphysician and mother on the Mendocino Coast, and has worked as an Intuitive Reader all over the world. She enjoys sharing stories of the paranormal highlights of her career, and interweaves memoir with tales of the eccentric English family that hatched her.

Janet Isaacs Ashford holds a B.A. in Psychology from UCLA and has been writing professionally since 1983. She is the author of two books on childbirth, seven on graphic design, numerous magazine articles, and one published short story. Her web site is jashford.com.

Cheri Ause lives in Gualala where she writes poetry, fiction, and creative non-fiction. Her work appears in at The Redwood Coast Review; Midwest Literary Review, real: Pure Slush vol. 3; and The Best of Every Day Poets Three (Spring, 2013) http://cheriause.blogspot.com/

Aron Lee Bowe's writing deviates from her extensive background in the visual arts. Since moving to the Mendocino coast, her focus is on memoir with the goal of turning her sad and boring life into a gut-tickling romp.

The writer in **Leatrice Callan** is the product of Bob Wynn, Suzanne Byerley, Charlotte Gullick and Norma Watkins. She has completed a novel, *MacDonalds of the Monach Isles*, and is searching for a publisher.

Standing in Gorda is **Tony Camarda**'s first book. It is a moment in interesting times, captured at a glacially manic pace. Tony has been writing and performing live theater for 20 years.

Why was Sophia/Wisdom severed from religious/political influence on the streets and royal courts in the ancient world? **Kathleen Damiani**, Ph.D., pursues the mystery on her web site: sophiaandthedragon.com. Her first foray into fiction is *Molly O'Brien & the Mark of the Dragon Slayer*.

Alena Deerwater writes fiction, creative non-fiction, poetry, dreams and imaginal explorations for Exterminating Angel Press: The Magazine (exterminatingangel.com). She is rewriting her young adult novel *Nightwriting: Enter at Your Own Risk* and working on a memoir *Anything but Normal*.

Molly Dwyer's debut novel, *Requiem for the Author of Frankenstein*, won the Independent Publishers Book of the Year Award in Fiction, and the Indie Book Award for Historical Fiction. She is the founding President of Writers of the Mendocino Coast.

Jan Edwards is a writer of political essays, with one published novel, a couple of short story awards and a dog named Victor Hugo. She struggles with metaphors from her home on the Point Arena ridge.

"Anthracite" is part of a memoir about **Charles Furey**'s early days. "Going Back" is his story of the Second World War. Works in progress include a story about the Coronado expedition, and another about a family traveling overland to California in 1861.

Gloria Schoofs Jorgensen, born in Atlanta, Georgia when it was still a small, racially divided town, began writing as soon as she could read. She has a degree from Goddard College in Plainfield, Vermont, lives in Point Arena, California, writes daily and attends College of the Redwoods.

Patty Joslyn writes more often than she flosses her teeth; she is fascinated by things such as laughter and shooting stars. She has eight self-published chapbooks and has been the featured poet/reader a number of times, in a number of places.

Malcolm Macdonald was born and raised in Mendocino County. He writes the weekly "River Views" column for the *Anderson Valley Advertiser*.

Jewels Marcus aspires to achieve bravery in brevity and often succumbs to the succinct. After 25 years of living in Oakland, she now loves living on the brink. "Writing poems is the most glorious endeavor," she thinks, "it's a rollercoaster ride mated with trapeze, Dizzy Gillespie and my shrink."

Lew Mermelstein is a new writer, having spent his previous career as an electrical engineer. He is working on a novel based on his experiences as a Peace Corps Volunteer in Ethiopia.

Neal Metcalf (Roy Neal) has a Masters from SFS and taught at Boise State. He is writing a memoir and a play about Hemingway. His play about Lawrence and Huxley has been produced in Point Arena, Taos, and Oceanside California.

Ginny Rorby is the author of four novels for young adults, *Dolphin Sky*, *Hurt Go Happy*, which won the American Library Association's Schneider Family Book Award, *The Outside of a Horse* and *Lost in the River of Grass*, a 2012/2013 Sunshine State Young Readers Award nominee.

Fran Schwartz moved from Los Angeles to Mendocino in 2005, consummating a forty-two year love affair with the North Coast. She writes memoir and creative nonfiction, published a memoir piece in *Woman's World*, and is currently working on a novel.

Marylyn Motherbear Scott writes memoir, makes poetry books, and offers featured readings. In publication: "Love's Journey" (poetry), "The Dragonslayer's Daughter" (fiction), "Rites of Passage" (nonfiction), "Gypsy Song for Calling the Dead" (invocation), Obama's Day of Inauguration (essay).

Nona Smith writes short stories and creative non-fiction pieces with a humorous twist, on the theory that everything can be seen through Groucho Marx's glasses. Really, if you try.

Holly Tannen is a folklorist and satirical songwriter. She wrote and performed a one-woman show, *Practical Alchemy: An Exquisitely Perverse Grace*. Her CD albums include *Rime Of The Ancient Matriarch*, *Crazy Laughter*, and *The Flower of Australia: Three Songs For Julian And His Friends*.

Norma Watkins writes and teaches writing on the Mendocino Coast. Her award-winning memoir *The Last Resort* is part of the Willie Morris Series in Biography. Her essays about the south and blogs on social justice are at www.normawatkins.com.

Honorable Mention

Katherine Brown
Stasha Ginsburg
Alena Guest
Joan Hansen
Gay Jolissaint
Steve Sapontzis

Non-Fiction

The Way Out

By Ginny Rorby

During a hellishly hot Miami summer, shortly after my mother was diagnosed with breast cancer, I took a beginning watercolor class. I'd envisioned a painting that expressed my love of the colors of fall leaves, mountains, and clear woodland streams, but I came away having gained no greater skill than I started with. I didn't blame the instructor. The fault was mine. I'd taken the class to stem a heat-induced restlessness, but because of my mother's illness, I couldn't stay focused. In the end, I painted a runny scene of a tree by a river against a backdrop of ashy-gray mountains.

Chemotherapy and radiation gave my mother a yearlong reprieve, but failed to stop the spread of the cancer and on my forty-fourth birthday her right hip—eaten away by the metastasized cells—crumbled under her slight weight.

The day of the surgery to replace her hip, I shared the waiting room with an old woman who sat with her eyes closed and her hands working around the tattered edge of a lace handkerchief. There was a painting on the wall—one of those cheap warehouse prints of red-jacketed hunters, their hounds, and a slaughtered fox. I viewed it with rising fury, as if I'd witnessed the kill. I hated the hunters and the baying, bloodthirsty hounds. The fox, chased down and torn limb from limb, had a trophy tail the color of my mother's hair before the poisoned strands came away in brittle clumps.

"Why would they have such a hideous painting on a hospital waiting-room wall?" I said aloud.

The old woman's hands stopped. She looked at the painting, then at me. "I've shared this room with it for months, and it reminds me," she said, "that dying is worse than death."

My urge was to argue the point, but I nodded out of a vague sense that I should—for her sake, and maybe for my own. I'd talked Momma into the hip replacement. She'd been on the verge of giving up. I'd also talked her into another round of chemo, but didn't tell her that it was a last-ditch drug, or that they were giving it in weak doses so as not to make her too sick. I filled us full of hopeful possibilities. My mother had no predictable lifespan left, but for however long she had I wanted to see her on her feet for it. I couldn't let the resignation of an old woman working her handkerchief like prayer beads knock me off my own frail footing.

I stared again at the painting and tried to imagine the person in charge of hospital waiting-room decor deliberately selecting it for its metaphoric message. It suddenly occurred to me that the decorator might have a sense of irony. Perhaps the laughing red-coated hunters were doctors and the fox a dead-goner of a patient full of tormenting chemicals and expensive replacement parts. I glanced at the old woman. Her eyes were closed again and her lips moved.

"Your husband?" I asked.

"My daughter."

"I'm so sorry."

The old woman nodded. "It's almost over."

I glanced at the clock, and back at the painting, drawn to it as if it were a crushing accident along a roadside. I recalled my watercolor instructor telling us that a true work of art should give the viewer a way in, a way out, a place to rest, and a place to hide. I'd turned back to my own painting and found the shade of the tree a good place to rest, the stream a way in, but I didn't see anything in it that provided a good place to hide or find—with all those ashy-gray mountains to climb—a way out.

My mother died within the month, before, I imagined, the shiny new rod, pins and socket had a chance to discolor. At the memorial service after her cremation, I kept wondering what had become of those spare parts. What—I wanted so badly to know—had become of all that appeared indestructible about my mother?

I took a week off after the funeral and drove to South Georgia. An acquaintance had a primitive cabin on the Satilla River, and I was grateful for the use of it.

The cabin was dark and dank, smelling of mouse urine, dust and mildew. I left the door open, propped the windows up with broom handles cut for that purpose and left it to air.

A few yards from the house, a fire ring held the remains of soot-covered beer cans, cigarette butts, shotgun shell casings and charred logs. A few yards beyond that was the edge of the bluff, twenty feet or so above the river. Standing at that point, I could see a quarter mile upstream and a hundred yards downstream to where the river slid by in an undisturbed silvery sheet, then doglegged left and out of sight. My preoccupation with the fate of those replacement parts of my mother made me see their shape and shine in other forms. In the hazy light of that afternoon, the river glinted like polished steel.

Both sides were tree-lined: pines and live oaks on the higher ground, bald cypresses at the water's edge looking as if they had waded into the wide curve of the river. It was fall, and their feathery green leaves had gone brown. I watched them tremble in the breeze.

I walked the bluff toward the bend in the river. At the point where I could see in both directions, there was a flat spot, dense with pine needles. That was where I would sleep, out under the trees and the stars.

The gunshot that woke me the next morning sounded so close I thought the pistol I'd brought to give me the courage to sleep alone outside had gone off inside my sleeping bag. With the second shot, I realized they came from the dense woods across the river. I rolled over, wrapped my pillow around the back of my head from ear to ear, and tried to escape back into my first trivial dream in months.

Instead, the painting on the hospital waiting room wall formed itself in the light behind my lids. I opened my eyes and watched the sunlight crackle and splinter through the cover of trees on the other side of the river, light the tops of ones on my side then slide from the tip of the branches down the trunks as the sun crept higher. Two more shots boomed, followed by a whoop of triumph. I got up and dragged my bedding back to the car, tossed the gun onto the front seat and went to the cabin to make coffee.

The woods lay quiet after the last shots. I wondered what had died as I carried a beach chair and my coffee down to the old live oak where I sat with my feet propped up on the trunk.

Sunlight splayed through the trees, warming miscellaneous patches of ground. The river was shrouded in mist, as if a ghost of itself lay along the same course as yesterday's live and moving stream. I couldn't see the water, much less its current, which left open the possibility that at sometime during the night the flow had ceased and its heart had stopped.

I'd only been sitting there a few minutes when I heard something in the water downstream. I dropped my feet, stood and shaded my eyes but could see nothing through the mist. The splashing started again, then stopped. From the woods across the river came the popping and snapping of branches breaking. I stepped behind the tree.

A boy about fourteen, dressed in overalls, a green and blue plaid flannel shirt, a camouflage jacket, and carrying a rifle burst through the thicket of palmettos at the edge of the woods and pitched off the sandy white lip of the embankment cut by a flood stage of the river. He landed on his knees, staggered to his feet and ran to the water's edge.

"Shit. Shit." He stomped the sand.

Down river, the splashing resumed.

"Pa," he shouted, shielding his eyes with his John Deere cap held toward the sun.

There was no answer from the woods, and the river went silent again.

"Pa. Are ya fuckin deef? Get the boat."

"What'd ya say?" A voice answered from the woods farther upstream.

"Get the fuckin' boat," the boy shouted, his face scarlet. "You stupid old fuck." He turned, scrambled up the embankment and crashed back into the woods.

Only after the shattered silence returned, did I hear labored breathing coming toward me. The mist still lay densely over the water so it was a bit longer before I saw the doe, mid-river, swimming against the current. Visible blasts of air came from her nostrils as she struggled to keep her head above water. When she saw the beach, she veered toward it, but, as if she'd seen the print of the boy in the sand, or smelled his having been there, she changed course and started for my side of the river.

She traveled diagonally with the current pushing against her. Offshore of where I stood behind the oak on the bluff, she touched bottom, staggered, then pitched forward. Her head disappeared below the surface. A moment later she came up snorting and dug her hooves into the footing she'd found. She dragged herself ashore using only her front legs.

I stood beside the tree, holding my breath so as not to frighten her back into the river. Though she'd ended up directly below me, she was out of sight because I was a few feet from the edge of the bluff. I backed toward the cabin and crept along parallel to the river until I could see where she'd collapsed in the sand. She lay on her right side, chest heaving, her hind left leg stretched lamely toward the water, her hip torn open to the bone. Blood seeped from the hole, staining her coat. The water, where it lapped and licked the wound, was the color of roses.

From downstream, I heard the rhythmic sound of oars slapping water. The doe heard it, too. Her head came up, eyes wide. Sand covered her right cheek, inexplicably reminding me of wet children and sand castles, Mom and me and my sister at Daytona Beach.

I ran to my car for the pistol, then back to a pine tree at the edge of the clearing. The sound of the oars had stopped and I could see them, the father holding the boat steady, his oars buried in the water, working back and forth against the current. They were downstream of the bend and hadn't seen the deer. The boy shielded his eyes against the light and scanned the banks.

The doe's front legs flailed the air wildly but she was dead weight on the sand. I walked down to the oak and looked over the edge at her. She saw me and we both heard the oars plow the water again. I waited with the gun held lightly at my side.

The boy saw me but not the doe. "You seen a deer swim by here?" he shouted.

I didn't answer.

"Is everybody deef?"

His father stared at me. "She heard you, boy." His oars worked to hold them steady in the current.

"How do you know? She ain't answering."

"That deer belongs to the boy, ma'am," the father said.

It was then the kid saw the doe. "Yeah, that there's my deer. I shot her, she's mine. Right, Pa?"

"Shut up, son."

I felt the weight of the .38 in my hand and realized that they thought I was planning to claim the doe. "I'm not going to let you kill her," I said.

The man looked too old to be the father of a boy that young. Fighting the current was wearing him out, and he turned the bow toward the opposite bank.

The doe, which had been quiet since she'd seen me on the bluff, began to kick again and tried to stand. The boy raised his rifle. I brought the .38 up and pointed it at them. "Put it down," I said.

"She ain't gonna shoot us," the boy said when his father reached and pressed the shiny barrel of his son's rifle toward the water.

"Maybe not," I said, "but if you don't get out of here, I'm going to ruin that boat for you." My heart battered the inside of my rib cage.

"Fuck you," the kid said.

His father slapped him in the back of the head. "I said shut up."

When the deer made a bleating sound and again tried to stand, I suddenly remembered that old woman in the waiting room. "Dying is worse than death," she'd said. I had to accept that I was as impotent here as I'd been throughout my mother's battle. This was death's M. O. Take a bite out of you and wait for time to finish you off.

For a moment, the father watched the deer struggling in the sand, then looked up at me. "I got seven kids, lady."

"Whose fault is that?"

"That there animal is suffering, and I got a family to feed. The boy here ain't the shot he oughta be, but it's done now and we'd be grateful if you let us go ahead and put her outta her misery." He rubbed his knees with both hands, then looked at his feet.

"Yeah," his son said.

The old man raised his hand again, but the boy flinched and hunched his shoulders. "Son, don't open your mouth again. This mess is your fault. You fired 'fore you had a clean shot." He looked up at me. "The lady's gonna do the right thing. She ain't gonna let that animal suffer. So just shut the fuck up 'til she's ready."

The doe was a blur through my tears. The scars her struggle had made in the sand reminded me of a one-winged snow angel. I looked out over the river, beautiful in the warm, white morning. When my mother quit her struggle, was it like this? A peaceful river with a soft, swift current to carry her away and out of my life?

"All right." I lowered the gun.

"I'm sorry, ma'am," the father said. He nudged the boy.

"Sorry," the kid muttered.

"So am I." I turned and walked to the cabin where the musty, mouse-piss smell soiled even the outside air. I sat with my back to the door jam and plugged my ears but still the shot that killed the doe was deafening.

I drew my knees up to hug and remained there in the dim filth until I no longer heard the splashing and the grunts of their labor to hoist the deer into the boat. When the river had been silent for a while, the birds began to sing and I realized I'd not heard them all day. I came out into the sunlight and walked to the edge of the bluff. All that was left of the doe was a rosy stain on the sand. There was no breeze, and nothing moved except a few insects like dust motes above the water and the flies on the bloody sand. Then for no reason, a cypress leaf dropped to the surface of the water and began to drift downstream. Walking the bluff, I followed it as it glided along in the current. It moved faster and faster until I had to run to keep up. I rounded the bend with it, broke through dense brush, and out into the open. Jelly-roll bales of hay lay about a field. I ran its length, occasionally losing sight of the leaf. I felt as if my heart would burst by the time I got to the fence, where I sank to my knees, hands gripping the wire between the barbs, and let my mother go. ❖

FICTION

Nightwriting: Enter at Your Own Risk

By Alena Deerwater

Collected from the private journal—now officially made public—of Willow "Star Wonder" Templeton

OKAY—THIS BOOK IS FROM THE ANNALS I kept during the summer Dad and I got back together—I mean, Dad and Momma got back together. I guess both are true, well, you'll see. I had just turned sixteen.

It all started when my momma, Crystal Amaryllis Templeton, got it up her butt that the only way she was gonna ever write a "book," instead of filling tons of notebooks, was if she went away.

"I just gotta be alone, be on my own for once, not taking care of anyone except myself," she said.

Dad and I didn't want her to go, but what could we do? We talked and talked and talked and then, *poof,* she was gone.

She told me—whenever I needed her, to write. It felt like a gift from a fairy godmother. Or maybe a curse. Only this was from my real mother and she was leaving me.

"Write, Star." She kissed my wet cheek. "Write, Star." And then the other cheek. "Write." Her lips landed last on my forehead. She looked me in the eye. "And do not waste time."

So I was abandoned, stuck for the summer with dear old Dad and Gammon, the dog.

I thought it would be a pretty boring summer, but three things started happening:

1 - Dad got all weird—secretive, disappearing, not being at work.

2 - Jimmy Clarke showed up in my basement one fine day.
3 - I started to write without the rules.

Friday, July 31 – sundown
SPIT IT OUT GIRL

As I hunker down among the long shadows on Momma's desk with this new notebook—unlined pages empty of words—as I finally pick up a pen Momma left behind and I am about to put it to paper, Dad comes in on his way to the observatory, flicks on the lights, and grounds me—just like that.

"I will call the house from work, young lady. You won't know what hour, what minute, what second of the night, but I will call. And if you are not home—or I hear Jimmy Clarke in the background—you can forget about ever seeing that boy again. He is not allowed anywhere near this house after the sun is below the horizon—sniffing around you in the dark of night. You hear me, Willow? No hanky-panky!"

I roll my eyes. Did he think I was deaf? How can you not hear a grown man having a hissy fit in your face? But by God, I got Dad to yell. It gave me hope in a weird way, you know, that things can change. Momma and I can't usually get a peep out of him, unless he's quoting Einstein.

I tilt back in Momma's desk chair, balancing on the rear two legs (I know this drives him crazy) and give Dad my meanest smile. You see, I'm not talking to my father anymore, and he knows it. So how can I answer the blasted phone?

"Just pick up the receiver and breathe into the mouthpiece," he says.

It's amazing how Dad can read my thoughts now that I'm not talking to him—now that I got his attention. I should of tried this years ago.

"If you don't answer the phone and breathe, Willow, I'll... I'll...I'll ..."

Looks like Dad's the one who needs to take a breath. He's sweating and his usually neat, thick black hair is sticking out like he's some over-aged punker from school. His skin's all splotchy. I've never seen Dad turn purple and red. He's always been such a paleface. Whew! I can even smell the heat rising off his anger. Man Alive! And he's still yelling up a storm.

"I'll… I'll… I'll dash home and whip your hide! I'll wrap my hands round your throat till I make you breathe, damn it, goddamn it, make you talk."

Well, my, my, my. What a way to coax a girl into talking. Now that I'm sixteen, Dad barely lays a hand on me, in violence or affection. Hasn't cuddled me in years.

"Spit it out, Girl." He explodes in my face.

How's it feel to be on the other side of this dark silence for a change, Bub? Without opening my mouth, I beam my thoughts directly from my blue eyes into his brown, and we freeze. Dad and I stare at each other in a moment of true silence. A pair of matching stones. He looks 'round Momma's writing room like he just realized where he is. I see him take in her desk, if you can call it that—an old door on top of a couple of beat-up wooden filing cabinets—her drawings and doodles and notes to herself tacked all over the walls, and books, tons of them. Momma read them all to me, starting when I was a wee thing. In the corner is a small bed, where neither of us were allowed to join her during her last few months in the house. She practically lived in this room by then. No one entered Momma's writing room day or night at that point; she made that perfectly clear.

Dad's shoulders slump a little and soften. He turns to leave, then pauses in the doorway.

"Please," Dad says to the empty hallway in front of him.

I can barely hear him. The chickadees on the maples outside the open window are louder.

"Willow… Star… talk to me, please."

God, he hasn't called me Star since I was a baby. But I can't talk to him now. I can't find words. I can't fathom what he's doing—to Momma—to me.

No. My eyes bore into the back of his head. *No.*

Dad smooths his hair down with his large hands. I watch his shoulders rise as he takes in a deep breath, re-erecting the fortress that he is. He straightens his suit.

How can he keep himself so covered up? It's a hot summer evening for God's sake.

He turns to me as if I had spoken, shoves the knot of his tie back up to his Adam's apple and says, "Do not leave this house."

WHAT A SHIT

I lower the front legs of the chair to the floor with a thump, reach over, and snap the harsh lights back off. Shadows embrace the room again. I listen as Dad clomps his way down the stairs.

I do not call him back. I do not follow him. I do not yell at his receding back: *Crap! Crap! Crap! I have never been grounded, I have never been spanked. So you whipping my hide is a bunch of bullshit crap! I renew my vow never to speak to you again. Unless, of course, you can get Momma to come back home.*

I concentrate on holding my jaw clenched tight as a vice. I feel the garage door going up, its electric motor shakes the room like a giant vibrator. Momma's writing room squats on top of the attached garage. I picture Dad banging the button with the palm of his hand instead of slapping me. I hope it hurts. I stare at my own hands, so unlike my Dad's large ones. I may have his thick black hair, but my hands have nothing to do with him, thank God. Oh, my fingers are long all right, but thin and tapered, delicate—not oversized and oafish like his. Dad's hands look like they were designed to whack something. I don't know what mine are made for yet. The station wagon revs up to get to the University before the stars appear.

The only way I know not to yell or speak is to write, but I find my hand has turned to stone along with my jaw. Only my ears remain alive and functioning. I listen. Dad backs out of the garage and pulls down the driveway, passing below the open window. He slows before turning onto the street.

I rise, dive to the window, finally booming out loud. "What's up your butt tonight, asshole?"

But Dad has hit the gas, and is already racing away to his precious observatory.

Besides, I know what's bugging him.

I walked by his bedroom earlier and heard him sweet-talking his new honey-love on the phone again: "Don't worry, Vivian…I know… It'll all work out. I have a plan. I'll tell Crystal everything as soon as she gets back home… I love you, too."

Can you fucking believe it? What a shit. My father, Walter P. Templeton, is a shit. I always knew he was a creep under his layers of precision.

ENTER AT YOUR OWN RISK

Writing is Momma's legacy to me. This notebook I am writing in, with it's recycled unlined pages, is one of hers. I found her stash in a cardboard box under her desk, right before Dad burst in and grounded me tonight. I hoped I'd found a treasure.

When I opened the box of notebooks, I thought—*Jackpot!*—Momma's journals. Even if I can't see her, speak with her, or curl up in bed with her at night, at least I can hear her words and listen to her stories. I stretched out on my back, right where I was on the floor, hugging the top journal to my chest. The underside of Momma's make-shift desk stared down at me, wooden door panels with an empty circle where the knob and lock used to be. No need for a key now.

Would Momma want me to read her journals? What would I find? Well, I'd seen the first pages before. At the beginning of every one of Momma's notebooks she writes a warning in huge letters—"ENTER AT YOUR OWN RISK." Then she sketches a Gorgon face like Medusa to protect her lifeblood's work. Momma'd glow all prideful red when she found one of her Gorgon drawings really fetching and show it to me.

Momma's kinda like Medusa, both before and after being cursed. Medusa was beautiful at first, did you know that? And so was Momma—long full red hair, pink glowing skin. Only when you were close enough to smell the heated earthy sent of her (no perfume or shaving for my Momma), did you notice her freckles and moles.

Looking at Momma's bare back is like looking at the stars in the sky. Tracing imaginary lines between her moles with my finger when I was little, I'd make up my very own constellations and stories to go with them. We would lie in bed together at night, trying to go to sleep in the summer heat or after a haunting nightmare. I'd tell Momma my stories and she'd tell me hers, creating our own new, ancient mythology.

I know they say Medusa's curse had something to do with a goddess, Athena or somebody, getting jealous—isn't that always the case with those old gods and goddesses? But I believe there is more to the story. I don't know anything about Momma's curse. She did get sorta mean and ugly. Come to think of it, maybe that's what first turned Dad to stone. What happened? Momma has told me so many stories, but not the ones I need to know. Maybe her writing will tell me.

I opened the first journal.

Blank.

No warning.

No Medusa.

Nothing.

I reached in the box for another journal and opened it.

Blank.

I opened another and another.

All blank.

I bolted upright to throw the goddamned empty notebooks against the wall and clobbered my head on the underside of Momma's door.

"Ouch! Fuck it! Fuck you Momma! Where the fuck are you? And what the fuck am I supposed to do with you gone!"

As if in answer to my cursing and questions, a pen spiraled down through the little doorknob hole in her desk into the box of empty journals.

Write, Star, write, Star, write and do not waste time.

The last thing she said to me.

I reached in the box for the pen, grabbed a notebook, and scrambled up into Momma's chair.

Maybe Momma's writing her guts out somewhere right now and thinking of me.

And then it hit me.

I'm going to write, too.

I, Willow "Star" Templeton, am writing.

For me.

No rules.

No boring book-ass assignments.

None of that crap.

I'd taken tons of writing classes in school. Did all the assignments—short stories, essays, book reviews, poetry, even a research paper—but I'd never written the way I feel like writing. No worrying about the goddamn rules, correct grammar, topic sentences, or even writing about what I'm *supposed* to write about.

Of course, that's when Dad had to bust in and ground me.

After I finished cussing him out and stomping around the room in semi-darkness, I curled up in Momma's little bed with the blessed pen and the empty notebook.

I opened to the first page.

I scrawled in huge passionate letters:

ENTER AT YOUR OWN RISK. ❖

"Point Arena Lighthouse," Janet Ashford

FICTION

The Rescue 1909

By Lea Callan

MURDOCH AWOKE SWIFTLY, his body tensing. Muffled shouts, faint but urgent, carried over the sounds of the wind hurling snow against the stone cottage. He threw back the covers, swinging his feet to the cold, plank floor. He grabbed his pants from the foot of the bed and was pulling them over long wool underwear when the pounding came on his cottage door.

"Murdoch! Murdoch MacDonald! Hurry man! She be going down!"

"Aye! Aye," he called back, recognizing Ewan's excited voice.

"Where are you, ye bugger?" he cursed softly, fumbling in the dark for his shirt.

Suddenly a soft, flickering light filled the small sleeping room, and Murdoch glanced around to see Ann placing the lighted crusie lamp on a table by their bed.

"Thank you, lass. I could'na find my way about. But dinna stir yourself, now. There's no need a'tall."

"No need, is it?" she said in a scolding voice. "And who'll be preparing your tea, Murdoch MacDonald, when you be coming in soaked to the skin?"

"There, now, mo'ghu," Murdoch spoke distractedly as he gathered his clothes, stopped momentarily at the sound of heavy boots clumping down the steep stairs from the loft. Through the doorway he could see Alec and Donald Archie hurry out the front door, letting in a gust of cold air. He guessed that they had not bothered to shed their clothes, damp from their watch on the beach, before falling asleep, preferring this discomfort to removing and donning them again.

Ann would brook no such peril to health for him, so he quickly pulled a warm, dry sweater over his shirt and drew sea boots over dry wool socks. He reached for the oilskins hanging on a peg by the door, turned before leaving the room, his eyes meeting Ann's for a moment.

"Dinna fash yourself, lass. The lads and I will be back in no time and wanting that hot cup'a. You'd best see to the fire." He hoped the homely activity would help keep at bay the stomach pains that afflicted her when danger from the sea threatened one of her brood.

He was gone and Ann shivered, pulling her shawl close about her against the icy draft of air. "Oh, aye," she murmured. "If you come back." With deep resignation, she closed her eyes and whispered a few familiar words. She wondered if the prayer uttered so many times still had the power to protect her men from the Old Girl when she was in a rage.

Through the long hours of night, the men of Heisker kept a rotating vigil on their rocky southwestern shore, and managed to keep a fire going in a storm that swept down from the icy fields of Greenland. It was a night that would normally see man and beast safely sheltered and locked against the unfriendly elements. But in the waning light of the previous day John Morrison, the joiner, had taken advantage of a slight lull in the storm to take an oar he made to replace a broken one in the lifeboat secured on Geo Eibrig, Little Fiord. There he saw what appeared to be a small merchant ship some distance from the shore. He judged it to be about two miles out and was surprised to see it so close to the island, far off the regular sea lane. Ships gave their island a wide berth, the danger of submerged rocks being far greater than from those that were visible, formidable though they were.

John continued to watch the ship for some moments, shielding narrowed eyes against the weather. It was making no headway but tossing aimlessly on the mountainous waves, at times almost dropping from view, then heaving into sight again. He guessed that the ship must have lost power and was now drifting in grave danger.

Urgency hastened his steps as he headed back toward the village. The wind was at his back as he crossed the white fields, his boots crunching in the fresh snow. The wind had picked up again and the driven snow found its way into his coat and ran in cold rivulets down his back. He went first to Murdoch's house to tell him what he had seen. Since receiving a medal of recognition, his third, from Queen Victoria of England For Gallantry In Saving Life in the rescue of survivors from the *HMS Columbus*, the unofficial mantle of captain in all rescue ventures had fallen on Murdoch's shoulders. They had also been supplied with a double-ender rescue boat, larger than the *Morning Star's* thirty-five feet and kept on the south-west shore, for it was off this part of the island that ships were most often in distress. They named it the *Queen Victoria*. John was relieved to find his friend at home, and Murdoch agreed to accompany him back to Little Fiord, instructing his two oldest lads to bring driftwood and hay, loose peat and a wee bit of kerosene with which to build a signal fire.

Now, many hours later, in answer to Ewin's call, Murdoch hunched against the bitter cold until he reached the rise above the beach. The snow-laden wind struck him with increased force. He shuddered, looked with dismay at the mountainous seas and strained to catch a glimpse of the stricken ship in the gray light of predawn. Shadowy figures moved about on the *Queen Victoria* still securely berthed on the beach, and Murdoch struggled to overcome dread at the thought of taking the *Queen* into such dangerous seas. Already a storm lantern had been secured in her stern to guide survivors and Murdoch knew that other essential supplies were stowed within the sturdy beams. The signal fire had served its purpose, letting the crippled ship know they were there through the night, ready to give whatever aid they could. It had early on responded with a flickering light. After the tragedy of the *HMS Columbus*, Stewart MacCuish asked for and received from the Home Office a signal light. With his rudimentary knowledge and the heaving of the ship, it was some time before he could decipher the message, the *Jorvic*. Stand by. Help on the way." After some discussion with his companions, he sent the message, "We are here."

Several times during the night the brief message, "Stand by," flickered through the dark to the men who stood in shifts huddled about the fire watching anxiously either for the light of another ship answering a distress call or from the *Jorvic*. In the dim light of dawn, though no signal had been seen, it was apparent to the men on the beach that the ship was in mortal distress, wallowing almost on its side, bobbing helplessly in mountainous seas.

Murdoch joined the men at the *Queen* and they immediately began to push it toward the surf. Mercifully, the tide was in so they didn't have to drag it across the worst of the rocks. When the water washed over their legs, Murdoch shouted, "Aboard then, lads." Stewart MacCuish, James MacAulay's younger brother, Cameron, Ewan MacDonald, Archie MacBryde, Alec Morrison and Murdoch's brother, Donald, hauled themselves into the boat, each taking his place on either side of the three cross beams, hoisting an oar to rest on the gunnel. Murdoch, too, entered the boat and took his place at the helm. Alec had volunteered to accompany his father, but it was understood that whenever possible, only one man from a family would take part in so hazardous a mission. He joined the remaining men in holding the boat against the next wave. Heaving mightily on the outgoing surge, the men retreated hurriedly as she floated and the men in the boat dipped their oars.

"Godspeed, Papa," Alec called.

"Aye, Godspeed to you," echoed the others.

On shore, the men shielded their eyes against the wind-driven snow and watched anxiously as the rescue boat lifted and plunged in the rock-strewn surf, struggling to make the open sea. They cut through the near waves where the storm's force resisted the pull of their oars. They were intent on avoiding the rocks in their path that could tumble them into the churning waters. They were soon drenched but paid little heed. It was a measure of their courage that not one among them could swim, the sea being home for fish and other creatures, but not so hospitable to men. As they left the shore further behind, the danger of being broken apart on the rocks lessened but was not absent, as Murdoch at the helm steered clear of submerged rocks he sensed but could not see. "Pull to the port, lads! Hard to the port! You'll no' be getting us this time, you sunken devils," he shouted. The Three Devils had left their mark on more than one boat. Now, their greatest peril lay in the huge rolling waves. They depended on Murdoch to accurately gauge the moment of cresting and to maintain control at the tiller as their small craft was seized and hurled over the mountainous waves. "Pull, lads! Pull!" He yelled each time they rode down a wave, only to be faced with another. It took all of their resolve to persevere in the face of such violence. They felt like a grain of sand caught in a hostile tempest. They kept their eyes on Murdoch, gaining relief from their fear in his resolute demeanor, his hand steady at the helm.

As they drew near where the freighter was last seen, Murdoch chose a moment when they crested on a high plateau. Shielding his eyes against the cold spray, searched the surrounding sea, he saw no sign of the ship they sought.

"Over there! Look! To the port, Murdo!" Ewan shouted as small pieces of timber and other debris passed their boat.

"She must be breaking up," Stewart yelled.

"Do you see her, Murdo?" Archie called.

"No' a sign. Look for survivors."

They descended into a deep trough and Murdoch wondered if any seaman could survive the icy water in such terrible conditions. Their boat could hold a maximum of fifteen besides the crew. He knew it would be enough. Only a fortunate few, tossed to the right place by the fickle whim of the Old Girl, would be counted among the living come full light of day.

"Pull, lads!" Murdoch shouted as their boat began to mount the next swell. Looking up he was stricken with terror to see the merchant ship towering over them, its deck tipped perilously. For a moment, the scene froze in time and Murdoch saw the small figure of the captain in full uniform, alone on the bridge, his body braced against the helm. In the next instant the ship skewed and its stern passed over them as they climbed the same wave it rode, almost swamping them with a deluge of icy water. Their boat was hurled up and then down into a deep trough and they struggled to stay upright in the turbulence left by the crippled ship.

They mounted the next wave. Looking back, they watched as the ship, its keel exposed, its stern in the air, disappeared into the sea. For a time they were numb with shock, stricken by a near brush with disaster and the sight of the sinking ship. Murdoch felt a deep loss. He knew the others, like himself, were chilled in spirit as well as body and feared the seething waters. He struggled to get his bearings and maintain control of the boat. "We've our job to be doing, lads," he shouted.

The men looked at him dully, their faces grim and unresponsive.

"We've a job just staying afloat," Archie shouted back.
Ewan began to bail water from the boat while the others mechanically worked the oars. Murdoch had seen the empty decks and hoped for survivors. His tall figure erect at the helm his voice carried strongly into the wind. "There are seaman out there, and little time to be finding them.

"Aye, Murdoch," Archie acknowledged stoutly, "You're right there."

"And look at the Old Girl, Stewart cried. "She's satisfied now. She's won her prize."

And indeed, the sea, as though sated and weary after the long struggle, calmed to rolling swells and no longer deafened the ears. Snow fell softly on numbed skin.

As visibility improved, they began to see the flotsam left behind by the steamer.

"Are you seeing any life boats, Murdo?" Cameron asked.

"Nay. But there are men afloat."

The men now plied their oars with powerful strokes. The first man they reached was clinging to the fo'csle boom. His eyes dulled by shock and the freezing water, he seemed barely alive as they hauled him into the boat. Ewen threw a blanket over him then returned quickly to his oar. Murdoch felt a great urgency to reach the other seamen who could be seen clinging to bits and pieces of wreckage and cargo.

"Pull, lads! Keep your oars deep. We've little time."

With desperate urgency and frustrating difficulty they reached survivors and hauled them, pale and shaking, into the boat. Four men clung to a hatch cover. One, little more than a boy, had the strength to grin briefly through blue lips and utter a few shaky words foreign to their ears. "Good lad," Cameron said, wrapping him in a blanket. "The good Lord was watching out for you this night." The last seaman they found was badly injured and appeared to be unconscious, even as they pulled him into the boat. The men set immediately to stanching the flow of blood from his head wound. They wondered how he had managed to cling to the timber that kept him afloat.

Twelve men in all were plucked from the frigid waters, and though the rescuers searched in the growing daylight, they found no others. Survival in the freezing water was no longer possible and their concern turned to the seamen sprawled in the wash of seawater at the bottom of the boat. All but the injured man had been given a dram of whiskey and were bundled in heavy woollen blankets, but their condition looked poor.

Once again the crew faced the hazardous journey between sea and shore. The men were exhausted and the boat heavy with its human cargo. Still they had no choice but to call on what strength was left to bring the craft safely home.

"It's a good night's work you've done lads." Murdoch spoke in a strong voice. "The sea's no' so fierce now. We've done all we can here. We'll be taking her in."

Buoyed up by this approbation and their confidence in Murdoch's ability to see them through the perilous journey, the crew lifted their oars. Murdoch was bone tired but knew he must keep vigil every moment of their return journey, must visualize where the rocks lurked beneath the surface in order to guide the *Queen* to shore. A mishap now could plunge not only his crew, but also the exhausted seamen they had rescued, into the turbulent offshore waters where there would be little chance of survival. He knew these waters well and steered a course with some confidence until, when almost past the danger, a rogue wave threw them sideways and they heard the ominous scraping of wood on rock. For a moment the boat was rudderless and tilted far to one side, shipping water.

"Pull!" Murdoch shouted as the boat scraped past the rock. "Pull!"

Sluggish with its load of men and water, the *Queen* slowly righted herself responding reluctantly as Murdoch struggled to bring it under control. The incoming waves carried them toward shore with oars divided between rowing and thrusting at rocks to keep the low-riding boat afloat until, with immense relief, they felt the keel dig into sand. The men on the shore beached the heavily laden boat as best they could. Others were already helping the surviving seamen. Murdoch dropped to the sea-washed sand where Ann waited with a dry blanket.

"Thanks be to God you're safe, Murdo." Ann spoke low, her eyes glistening. "I thought my heart would be stopping when it seemed the boat would be tipping you into the sea."

"Aye, it was bad then and worse out there. We watched the ship going down, Ann. It's no' a thing I'd want to be seeing again."

"Here now, you're shaking." She tucked the blanket more securely around him and urged him to the fire. "I'll be giving you a hot cup'a to be taking the chill off." She would like to have hugged him and taken him home right then, but she knew such a display would embarrass him and he would not leave until the boat had been firmly secured. He squeezed her arm briefly as they walked toward the fire.

"Aye," Murdoch spoke reflectively. "We should all be thanking God this day for putting our feet on solid ground again. It's a thing those poor devils who went down with the ship will no' be enjoying again."

"Hush, now. Think of all these men you were saving."

"Aye, there's that."

By now the women and children, all but the oldest and youngest, gathered at the beach. They brought dry blankets and brewed strong hot tea over the fire. The fire and the tea offered wonderful warmth to the cold and exhausted men. The injured seaman was placed on a blanket with the four corners tied to sturdy poles to form a makeshift litter. Another blanket was tucked around him and a clean white cloth wrapped around his head before he was carried to the cottage of Janet MacQuarrie. Soon they were walking across the snow-covered field toward the cottages. Now the women were in command and each family took charge of one or two seamen, enveloping them with warmth and charity. ❖

Non-Fiction

Secrets

By Fran Schwartz

DRIVING SOUTH ON WESTERN AVENUE in my '87 Civic, I checked the door locks. William's Aunt Davina lived in the middle of a tired block, in a building with peeling gray paint, broken blinds and withered grass. A '75 Chevy without wheels slumped at the curb. The street petered off into a dead end where a clump of men stood around an overflowing trash-can, waiting. Maybe the dealer was late.

It was April, 1994. In the 10 years since my godson shivered into the world, scrawny and quaking from cocaine, he had lived in five homes. Nurtured for six years by his elderly great aunt and uncle in Compton, he later moved with his mother to Long Beach. By age eight, he had attended three funerals and begun his migration from aunt to aunt.

Davina, Aunt Number Three, was not an improvement. A recovering addict, she lived with her boyfriend and several of her children in a cramped apartment. Hyperactive William had worn out his welcome with two of her sisters.

I parked and navigated the front walk, littered with crushed Budweiser cans and flyers for a nail salon. The dingy stairwell reeked of mold and garbage. Davina's sagging screen door was locked. A TV blared. I rang until William bolted to the door.

"Fran's here!" He unlatched the lock and threw himself into my arms. He knew we were going to the circus and looked sharp in new clothes—a Magic Johnson shirt and black jeans.

Davina emerged from the bedroom, dressed in a faded housecoat and worn slippers. Barely 40, she looked ground down. The dark circles under her eyes and slight trembling of her hands unnerved me. Her four-year-old son bounced around, tugging my sweater, begging for treats.

I pulled a pack of Trident from my purse. "OK to give this to Lamar?"

She reached for the gum and pushed him behind her. "*You* wait until after lunch. Stop bothering Fran, she needs to go." She seemed anxious to get me out the door.

William hopped up and down. "Take a jacket," I said. "It will be air conditioned."

As we drove to the Los Angeles Sports Arena, I described the animals and acrobats we would see. I liked to open William's mind, to expand his narrow world. We parked in a sprawling lot and walked through the crowds toward the entrance. A balloon vendor with a clutch of metallic balloons hawked his wares in English and Spanish. The aroma of hot dogs and popcorn permeated the air. William gripped his ticket, eyes wide with excitement.

Inside, I navigated toward the refreshment stand. "Order whatever you want, but we won't come back after the show—no extra snacks." I always spelled out what we would do, what I would and wouldn't buy. Otherwise, William sulked and threw tantrums. I had learned the hard way about limits. As we moved toward our seats, a young father hoisted a bawling toddler by the arm and swatted him on his rear.

"That's *enough*, or we're going home."

The child sniveled as the dad pulled him down the aisle. William froze.

"Sometimes parents get impatient," I said. "It makes me uncomfortable, too." I patted him on the shoulder and he flinched.

I located our seats, not as close to the center as I'd requested, but with good views. William wolfed a cheeseburger and dipped his fries in a packet of catsup. He sucked noisily on a strawberry shake, and in three minutes had demolished his lunch. He was always ravenous.

Once I peeked into an aunt's fridge and found only Pepsi, two slices of baloney and a jar of mayonnaise.

We flipped through the pages of the glossy souvenir program while I pointed out pictures of clowns, tightrope walkers, and trained sea lions. The lights dimmed and music swelled. I squeezed William's hand. An emcee in top hat appeared in the center ring, declaiming in sonorous tones. "Ladies and gentlemen, we proudly present.... ."

For the next two hours William focused on the spectacle, pointing to elephants and tigers, and gasping as acrobats flew through the air. He jabbered excitedly, sometimes jumping out of his seat. Closing my eyes, I drifted back to 1949, when I was 10, surrounded by my parents and older brother, breathing cotton candy and elephants at Madison Square Garden. Safe, loved, and innocent—the inverse of William's world.

When the show ended and we strolled to the car, William dragged his feet, deflating like a balloon. I unlocked the door and he slid into his seat. He pressed his nose against the window, staring at the cars in the parking lot.

"Did you enjoy the circus? What did you like best?"

No response.

"What's wrong?"

I turned off the ignition, locked the doors and put my arm around his shoulder. He shrank from my touch. Gently, I turned his face toward me and then spotted the red welt under his shirt collar.

"There's a bruise on your neck."

He pulled away, tugging on the collar.

"You can tell me, I won't be angry. Did you fight with one of your cousins?"

He shook his head, chin on his chest. "Davina's boyfriend," he mumbled.

I glanced around, feeling exposed in the car. My hand curled into a fist but I mustered a casual tone.

"What happened?"

"He was mad 'cause I wouldn't turn off the TV." William lifted his head. His eyes welled with tears. "I just wanted to see the end of the cartoon. He grabbed me 'round the neck and twisted. When he dropped me, I run to the bedroom but he chased me. He took off his belt..." He faltered. "... and whupped me. I screamed and Darrell saved me." His voice flattened, devoid of emotion. A solitary tear trickled and I brushed it away.

Davina's oldest son Darrell was 18, tall and muscular. The nameless boyfriend probably didn't want to mess with him. My throat contracted. "Does Davina know he beat you?"

"She knows, but she's afraid. He's mean when he's usin'." His offhand tone twisted my gut. He grabbed my hand. "You can't tell. Don't say nothin'. It's a *secret*." His voice dropped to a whisper. "Promise, Fran, promise."

My mind reeled. Confront Davina? Tell Aunt Germaine, whom I respected? If I told, would he ever confide in me again? Would his family allow me to see him? If I didn't tell and the abuse continued....

I took William's hands. "If I don't say anything, he might hit you again. I can't let that happen. Friends take care of each other, and you're my special friend." I turned the key and put the car in gear.

He yelled, "It's a secret. If you tell, we ain't friends." He slid toward the window and punched the radio buttons, searching for his favorite rap station.

That night I woke in a sweat from a nightmare. William screamed, drowning at the bottom of a well, and no one heard him. Since his mother's death two years ago, I had struggled to establish rapport with his aunts. Initially wary and uncertain of my motives, they had gradually accepted me. I wasn't a social worker but a friend, like a kindly aunt or grandmother. Since I wasn't prepared to offer William a home, I couldn't sit in judgment. His family lived in a different world, coping with too little money and too many kids in gang-infested neighborhoods. I should report the abuse but feared repercussions for William. Would his family take it out on him? Would they cease to trust me?

A week later, Aunt Germaine called. "William just moved to my sister Adele's in Inglewood."

Reprieve. I exhaled deeply. "What happened?"

"His teacher reported some bruises. We found out Davina's boyfriend Joe was beating up on the kids, not just William, but Lamar too. Davina lost custody of her kids--they're living with my sister, Chantel. Davina's in rehab and Joe's in jail."

I thanked her and dialed Adele's number.

Aunt Number Four. ❖

FICTION

Moby Jane, Princess of Whales

BY HOLLY TANNEN
DEDICATED TO GREG GRATHAM

"GET OUT OF THE CAR," says Jeannie, my wicked stepmother.

"Rachel, this is your last chance," says my Dad. "Ten…nine…eight…"

I bang my laptop shut and shove it into my backpack. "I'm gonna get seasick."

"No, you won't. Jeannie packed ginger candy and we're renting you a wrist band."

"Where's your jacket?" says Jeannie. "Your hat?"

Dad says, "Did you remember your gloves?"

There's nothing in Moss Landing 'cept a power plant with two huge chimneys. A bunch of old people with cameras and backpacks stand around waiting to get on the boat. Little yappy kids, but only one boy my age.

When Dad lived with Mom we'd go to movies and concerts. Jeannie always wants to be as uncomfortable as possible. We go to the desert and get sunburned; we go to the mountains and freeze; we sleep in tents and get wet; we pee outside and get bit by mosquitoes. She always says, "You're going to love this," and I always hate it.

The Sanctuary is a dinky white boat. The captain tries to take my arm when I get on, but I won't let him. The boat lady puts a band on my wrist that sends pulses to my brain so I won't puke. She wants me to wear a life jacket. I tell her I don't have to, I'm twelve, I can swim. She says everyone under fourteen has to wear one. She pulls this orange thing over my head and straps it across my chest.

How come I have to do Monterey Bay again? I did it for a whole moon-cycle. Mother says, that's what happens when you don't come to council. If you'd take part in the decision-making, you might get what you wanted. Would you rather be up in the Bering Strait freezing your blubber off?

The captain says the bay is full of huge swarms of underwater earwigs. The whales gulp them down and swim to Hawaii to make babies. Dad nudges Jeannie and whispers in her ear. If they make a baby, I am never going to spend the weekend with them again.

The boat heads out from the dock. The water is greasy and smells like gasoline. There's rows of big black birds sitting on pilings. Dad points out a seal in the water, watching us.

"I've seen those." I go into the cabin, squeeze behind the table, and pull out my laptop.

It's not my fault I didn't go to council. I'm coming into season and the boys are all over me, rubbing up against me, stroking me with their flippers. Mom says, swim upside down. But I have to breathe, and soon as I roll over, whomp, one of them gets me.

Dad sticks his head into the cabin. "Come look at the sea otters. They swim on their back and crack shells on their tummy with a rock."

"Saw it on the Discovery Channel. Can I have a candy bar?"

"Your mother said one a day."

"You drink beer."

"That is a whole 'nother conversation."

"You smoke pot. You have sex with Jeannie."

Dad's face gets red. He grips the sides of the cabin door.

"Rachel, why do you have to act like this?"

"I am being deliberately annoying."

What if I could choose the father of my calf? Aroha is the handsomest. He has scalloped white flukes with dark spirals. Luru knows more songs than anyone, and sings them louder. Migaloo is pure white, but he lives off the coast of Australia. He's southern and I'm northern; the babies wouldn't know which way to swim.

Mother says, go for the smartest. Everyone thinks that's Kahu, but I don't. He just has the biggest mouth. He tells everyone he invented bubble-netting, but I know for a fact he learned it from his mother.

The motor gets louder and the boat speeds up. We're out of the harbor now, and there's nobody in the cabin but me. I tiptoe up to the snack tray and take a bag of M&Ms.

I wouldn't mind a moon cycle at Bodega Bay. There's just two watcher boats. Most of the monkeys stand on the cliffs, so you can't hear them. And you only have to do high tide, so you have lots of free time.

Mother says, I've been watching them for twenty years, and I've never seen one poop. Then I realized that's what the big box on the boat is for.

And they say we're weird because we have to think when we want to breathe.

The problem with Bodega is the grays. I am not prejudiced, but they are kind of primitive. They're bottom-feeders, they lie on their sides and suck mud. It makes their baleen lopsided. And they're covered with lice.

Here comes Dad again. He steadies himself against the door-frame, and carefully steps over the transom and through the cabin door. He hunkers down next to me. "Dolphins!"

Sighing like Scarlett O'Hara, I close the laptop and follow him out. People in sweatshirts and down jackets are lined up at the rail with cameras.

Monterey Bay is, pardon my language, a zoo. Big boats, little boats, full of monkeys jumping and hollering every time you take a breath. The boats aren't supposed to chase you, but they do. I lost weight last time, if you can believe that, even though the bay was full of krill and we chowed down sixteen hours a day.

Oh no, here come the dolphins, dippy little show-offs, and their buddies the sea lions.

"That's called porpoising, when they jump into the air," says Jeannie. "The sea lions learn it from the dolphins."

"Those aren't dolphins. They have square heads?"

"Flipper on TV is a bottlenose dolphin. These are Risso's dolphins. Doesn't it look like they're wearing eye make-up?"

"They're all scratched up."

"They eat squid, and the squid fight back. Imagine if your pork chop fought back. Look—under the prow."

Dozens of thin black and white dolphins crisscross in front of the boat. One leaps into the air and slaps his tail three times on the water before splashing back in.

Those monkeys are always going on about how big their brains are. And what do they do with their big brains? Think up new and better ways of destroying themselves and everyone else. They can't even figure out how to keep warm without killing other animals. Though Mother says in the last fifty years they've put on a lot more blubber.

Dad says, "We're going twelve knots and we can't outrace them."

"How do they do that, Dad?"

"They're all muscle. And they aren't distracted by taxes and car repair and divorce."

Mother, I said, it is demeaning to keep jumping out of the water like that. I feel ungainly when I make a big splash and all the monkeys scream and giggle.

She says, think of your grandchildren. Do you want the old days back? They'd kill your baby, and when you swam up to help it, they'd kill you. She has told me this story a thousand times.

The dolphins and sea lions swim off. In search of fish, the captain says. It's windy up here. I wish I had my scarf. We're in the middle of Monterey Bay and I can't see land anywhere.

I wish Mom could see the dolphins. I wish Mom and Dad didn't hate each other.

Look at it this way, Mother says. When the monkeys hoot, the orcas don't come round, and if they do, you can hide under the boat until they get bored and go bother someone else.

A boy in a Cal Tech jacket comes up and stands next to me. He's skinny, with gold-rimmed glasses and dark hair he keeps pushing out of his eyes. "I'm Jeremy. My Dad's a marine biologist. This is my third time. Wanna try my binoculars?"

"There's nothing to see."

"There will be. Know how to focus them?"

Mother says, get as close as you can, stay as long as you can, and make eye contact if you can, especially with the young ones. Push the edge of your comfort zone. Remember, the monkeys in the boat aren't the ones who killed our parents.

A woman yells "Eleven o'clock." Everyone rushes up front.

"Thar she blows!"

What are they screaming about? There's mist on the water is all. Then I see the spout.

I told her, I'm already out of my comfort zone. My comfort zone is Hawaii. That's when she whacked me with her fluke.

I see a gray back rolling in the water, then a little fin. A black and white tail with a chunk missing flips up and slowly sinks back down.

"It's a humpback," hollers the captain.

Okay, I'll swim alongside, but I am not going under the boat.

One time I got within a hundred yards. Sori and Jolene and I dove down and came up together with our mouths open. Shoulda heard 'em scream. One of 'em goes,"Oh God! Oh Lord! Oh my God!"

Weird religion.

The whale is surrounded by dolphins. They swim beside the boat real slow. The whale gives a giant snort and I jump back. Whale snot smells like rotten fish.

Hey, dolphins, get out of here, this is my gig. I didn't swim all the way out here to be upstaged by a bunch of groupies.

The whale rolls over on its side and looks up. Its eye is gigantic. It looks at us. We look back. Everyone is silent. Then the whale turns slowly right side up. The whale and the dolphins swim away.

Jeremy says, "She is the Princess of Whales, and those are the knights, her escorts."

The captain turns the boat around. He puts her in high and the prow rears up out of the water. Me and Jeremy sit in the cabin and Dad brings us hot chocolate.

Okay, I did it. Satisfied? Gave me the creeps.

Dad drives me home and drops me off at the door.

"How was it?" says Mom.

"Best day of my life. There were dolphins—they swam faster than the boat. And a humongous whale came right alongside."

"Wow. You're lucky. How about a nice hot bath?"

She comes into the bathroom with towels warm from the dryer and puts them on the shelf.

"What did the Wicked Witch of the West do today?" she says.

"Nothing."

Mom gives me a look and walks out. I lie in the bathtub blowing bubbles. I wonder what it's like to live in the ocean. I wonder what it's like to be a whale.

It looked me right in the eye. ❖

Author's Note: The story of the young boy and the Princess of Whales was told to Dick Russell by Heidi Tiura of Sanctuary Cruises, and is printed in his book *The Eye of the Whale: Epic Passage From Baja to Siberia*, p. 244.

Non-Fiction

Finding Myself in York

By Neal Metcalf

IMAGINE HAVING AMNESIA. I had always thought it an overly used concept, an artificiality of movies: a man cannot remember who he is; an afflicted woman screams, "He is not my husband!" And then it happened to me. Is this worth telling? After all, I lived it.

But I did find out, yet again, how close to the surface, how near to hand, lay my old panic, chuckling to itself with infinite patience. It is almost as old as I am.

It happened like this: my eldest daughter is driving me and two grandsons to see York, the old town of Richard III's puzzling and converging streets. The eldest grandson is in the front acting as navigator—reading the GPS. "In point three miles, Mom, exit to W52. When you come to the roundabout, you will enter at six o'clock, take the exit at two o'clock." Greek to me until twenty turns later. "This is the street, take a right and door is on your left." He looks up. "We should be here." And so we are.

We go in and the lady receives us kindly. I have my bag, and pillow under-arm. "Greetings. You will be in the two rooms on the third floor, but you are early. Check-in is not for two hours. You may leave your bags here and I will keep an eye on them. Just go down (she holds out her palm) this way, take a left at the corner." The pleasant innkeeper tells my daughter how to take the stairs that go up to the old wall that once encircled the modest Castle of Richard the Third. "It's a lovely walk to get your bearings, and you can go down on the other side, or anywhere you wish."

We do as suggested, with me cheerfully tagging along, one of my grandsons in hand. "I can't believe that GPS," I announce.

My grandson gives me a smile. "Oh, Big Daddy." He speaks sympathetically. His childhood is nothing like mine, and I am glad. Childhood has "evolved," and my eldest daughter gave me the kindness once of suggesting that, although she and her sister were "damaged," it was probably not as damaging as I had known, as each generation improves. She is a wonderful mother: a rock of dependability. I did not have a rock. I had to be the rock. It plays hell with your childlike sense of wonder, as some author has observed. (Cheever?)

At 11, I was raising a family. At 12, I was more or less a man. At 13, I worked until midnight and worried about getting the rent paid on time. Keeping my mother alive and sane was my pre-occupation. It wasn't as bad as the childhood of a Dickens character. Society had evolved beyond a childhood of out-right slavery. We owe that to Queen Victoria, who decreed, "All children will go to school", and so invented childhood by giving it a structure beyond work.

The old wall is somewhat interesting, where archers protected the humped-king who dwelled within, with slits in the masonry just wide enough to shoot arrows through, but not big enough to create a danger to the archers. And so we walk in a circle around, and go down a stairway to the street, to see a sign that says, "The city that invented chocolate." We soon learn that for reasons unknown, they no longer make chocolate. I must say something sarcastic, and we are tired from the drive, for my daughter points: "See that museum, Dad? Why don't you go in there and I'll take the boys to find something they like." (The top of a Ferris wheel twirls in the distance.) "Go on, Dad. You've got ten pounds and we'll see you in a couple of hours, or back at the rooms."

It sounds like a good idea—get a break from each other after the confines of the car, get over my poor performance at the last overnight stop, in the Nottingham area, where I mentioned the lack of a fan and the impossible shower. (I was right about the shower. I should be acquitted on that count, but sometimes, no matter how right you are. You know the saying, "Do you want to be right, or do you want to be—?" I forget how it goes.)

"Righto, I'll be fine in here, or over at the other museum. Look, there are two museums." I wave goodbye and add, "Don't worry about me."

(Even though I know better than to say things that are optimistic.)

So, I have a couple of hours to learn about York, and to find something referring to my family name—a name that "came from York," someone said.

I'll find myself, I announce within, in my poetic, bullshit way.

And I was curious about the story of the questionably clairvoyant woman whom they hung from the bridge over the River Ouze. (I am always drawn to the tragic, and other things I've completely forgotten, due to …)

Well, why don't I tell you *What happened next,* as writers like to say, though it's a little embarrassing.

I wandered around in the first museum, the ho-hum rusty relics of Romans, the utensils and ceramics dug-up from the Nordic invasion, the olde maps, the knowns, the educated guesses. In fact, there was a map on the very floor on which I walked, showing me the Island (Britannia), the Towne (York) which Romans made the Capitol, more important than London, in olden days, the likely routes of this, that, and the other. (Seinfeld is always rolling around in my head.)

I spent three pounds on the entry fee, and had a Coke with another pound as I rested from the exhausting leisure of enjoying a museum. There were books and such for sale, but I lacked the pounds. So I bought a postcard, and realized I had no one to send it to.

I could write something funny, but not everyone appreciated my humor. When I do my impersonation of "What About Bob?" they don't always laugh. "Good morning, Gil (the goldfish), I say. "Good Morning! Gil." Then I tap hard on both temples, saying, "I feel good, I feel great, I feel wonderful … I feel good, I feel great, I feel wonderful …" I look in terror at the apartment door—big gulp, and begin with the many locks, in hand gesture, so funny…You had to be there.

But I digress. Realizing I didn't have any energy left for the second museum (the Coke didn't take), with two hours mostly blown, I left (And I was satisfied that religious zealots had hung the poor woman because it was time to hang a woman. God spake.)

I took a little walkway to the east—no, west—and meandered into the old blackened slabs of a chapel, went around to the front, found it open, and looked around at the stained glass. I'm startled by an organ and I thought of Virginia Woolf, who said somewhere, "as the organ *complained.*" (I must have liked that.)

I made my way to the back, where many volumes of very old books lay open, under glass. Maybe fifteen books, eighteen inches long, were lined, and signed with legible names, dating to 1237… 38, 39, A.D. I began to read them, fascinated.

And there I was.

Simple as that. In York. My name. My ancestor. In careful scroll was the proudly ornate: '*Willeum Corneilius*'—waiting for me to find.

I had learned long ago that 'Neal' was an extract from Corneilius—and I smiled. And looked—and smiled again—read more books, went back to it—smiled again, and then saw, unbelievably—*Mary Royle!* (I go by 'Roy', but it's actually Royle.)

Obviously Will and Mary got together—and looked forward to a baby boy.

I needed a few centuries to get myself ready, but I must have finally felt the time was right, for I had daughters I needed to give to the world. And some grandchildren, with a better shot than my daughters had—better than I had. Though I am beginning to feel, with age, I had a better shot than I like to complain about—accompanied by da-doom of Virginia's "complaining Organ."

Satisfied that I had found my origin, I headed straight into the tangled web of streets leading back in the direction from which we started.

41

I have a good sense of direction, except for north and south—sometimes east and west. (I think you'll agree that all people are dyslexic in some way or another.)

But even with my good sense of direction, nothing seems familiar. Finally, in my best false-self-deprecation, I ask the kindly face of an older woman which way I should go, only to realize, in dismay, I have no words to formulate the question, like which street I am looking for, or what the name of the B&B is… for I wasn't paying any attention when my daughter, with grandson riding shotgun, deftly wound through town and deposited us at the door. North? South? Who needs them? "See three parking spaces on your left, take any one of them." Traveling was different forty-five years ago when I was eighteen—no car, a torn map, no GPS.

Familiar panic begins to seep into my doomed emotional life. Thanks, Corneilius.

I gasp to a total stranger: "There was—a stairway—up to that wall."

"Well, sir, there are five of those stairs. You don't know what street it was?"

I back away. I'm a lunatic.

I walk for another half-hour, in panic, sweating, and squander my pounds when I see a chocolate shop, a franchise. Desperate to do something normal I make a simple purchase, palming-out the remainder of my unfamiliar coins.

"You don't know the name of the street you live on?" the shop-girl replies, in the wake of my fake laugh. She puts into my palm the larger and least valuable of currency.

"No, I don't know which street I live on, or the name of the place, or any address, or any phone number, just a cell phone that doesn't work here. "I got nothing" as my grandsons like to put it." She laughs at my humor. See? I'm not crazy.

Several people wish they could help, but "There aren't any B&Bs near here. This is all residential. Try over that way about four blocks."

So I keep walking, my mind like an abstract painting I don't understand—a clock in meltdown, limp as a pancake.

I am a man on the edge of losing it. I take anything as a sign of hope. When an attractive woman approaches, I straighten-up and take a more confident stride, as a completely sane Yorkian might do, disguising my near lunacy, and pulling myself back from the edge. I nod, all is well. I am still in the ballgame, as my last doctor put it.

I must hang on. I know nothing except that I walked up some stairs to get to the wall—but which ones? I was just following along. Face it, you are lost. And your daughter will kill you if you ever see her again.

I am lost in York, where my own ancestors would simply laugh and fall into a haystack over my desperate concern. "After all, Laddie, it is only a sexually transmitted condition called Life. It is simple. You give a woman your sperm, she hands you back your son."

And you can put him to work laying down cobblestones to make streets into a curving and converging maze—or constructing the leaning shops called "The Shambles"—where the buildings are held up by the ones next to it, all ready to tumble forward into the street.

But, since all the streets are a sea of people from all over the world, it said something about doing things the "right" way. Had everything been done along the straight and narrow, where would be the quaint attraction?

But its quaintness is wasted on me as I stumble on.

I feel good, I feel great, I feel wonderful.

This wilderness of people and swerving cobblestones speak strange languages—until I have, I have—yes! I have a brainstorm.

Had I not passed a place that looked like a B&B?

My wheels are turning like crazy, as I turn back, my mind rattling over the cobblestones with a new music.

Would a found B&B be willing to help an "olde Yorksman?"

Of course she would—after chastising me for not staying at her place.

"What is the name of it?" she asks, smiling at my unnecessary suffering, which she is about to rescue, no problem "a-tall," which is the way we Brits talk.

"Oh—I'm not sure … if … I can …"

The smile begins to disappear from her friendly face. I'm not "having-her-on," am I?

"Really, I don't know the name—It might have had the word 'gate' in it, maybe."

She 'clucks' like a mother hen, but believes me. An American having-her-on would not look this disheveled and un-done.

She dutifully exhausts all the Gates in the phone book.

She asks me to wait while she checks in the arriving people, who "do know" where they are staying. They are staying at her place—"the best place" in town. I believe her.

I am lucky to have met a patient and kind woman willing to care about a stranger. If I live, I may return to York, just to stay at her place.

"I will ring a friend who has a place a few blocks over."

Nothing comes of it.

I am still lost, in the very spot on the globe where my people were found.

But I hear a voice going down the street and run outside. I hear my daughter!

The startled woman quickly backs away from me—the madman—she isn't my daughter. I slump back into the house I have adopted as my home.

"I'll get you a glass of water," my savior says. "You don't look very well."

A picture of Jesus on the wall looks very much like her, except for the beard.

I am a man who doesn't know who he is, his only identification in his lost luggage, a ha'pence in his pocket, no idea where he lives, what street, phone number, or what the Guest House is called.

This must be getting boring for you, so I will cut to my savior's next call, a list of guest houses she repeats aloud—and I recognize a name she utters.

"That's it! That's the one. I think so."

She calls The Bowman House, and yes, they are looking for a lost traveler.

My daughter insists they send a car for me. I can no longer be trusted to walk three blocks on my own, to Gladstone Street—turn right to the first door on the left (It wasn't "Gate" I saw briefly, subconsciously, but "Glad".).

Exhausted, barely able to push myself out of the car seat, I am just in time to walk back to town for dinner, but lighter of heart—passing the very establishment where I had only minutes before been found, and simultaneously lost a few years of my life.

I am asked (told) to promise that I will never get out of my daughter's sight again.

"All right."

"I want to hear 'Yes.'"

"Yes, sure, okay. I will stay in sight of you."

When we are all seated in an Italian restaurant, I am giddy with gladness—I try a conversational theme. "Did you know, boys, that Mr. Gladstone was the rival in Parliament for the graces of Queen Victoria? Oh yes, boys. Disraeli, I think it was, fell in and out of besting Mr. Gladstone, as they each became Prime Minster, more than once, as I recall."

No one takes me up on my conversation. We study the menu. I am thinking, and having my own conversation with myself. Why should I feel bad about this little mishap? Why should I live in fear, as if I were a two year old lost in a train station? What can happen? What else can go wrong? (Quickly, I delete that question.)

But I make a promise to myself. I will no longer live in fear.

I look up from my menu, to check my daughter's steam factor.

That is the term we have given her mood.

To prove my new-found courage, I ask, "Can I go to the bathroom?" (I have aged in the last four hours beyond my years. Old guys have prostates.)

She looks up from her menu, turning it over in her mind, as if I might be planning an escape. The table falls silent (a beat) and the boys stop breathing while the jury is out.

The oldest boy breaks first, and in a sympathetic breath, he says, "Oh, Big Daddy."

"Hey, I didn't 'mean' to get lost." I laugh, but no one joins me.

The younger brother quietly whispers, "Don't push it, Grando."

"In fact, daughter, I found something interesting in a church." She doesn't look up.

I decide to save it for the ride home to their Air Force housing.

Finally, my daughter relents, and gives instructions, to the youngest boy on my side of the table, to go with me, and to, "Take him by the hand."

Whole tables turn to watch us, looking to see if I am handicapped. (They have no idea.)

I am led by my grandson to the bathroom door, where he stands guard.

Leaning my forehead into the wall, I sigh, I wait, I breathe with relief, waiting to feel the weak stream of further relief.

I have seen the town of York, my olde home towne, have looked for the origins of myself, successfully. These ancestors may not want to admit they know me—my daughter doesn't at the moment, but she and my other daughter, expect me to come through with these moments of buffoonery. I am known to break the unbreakable, like a golf cart. I trip and fall on the stairs with arms full, but save the eggs. It is both expected and appreciated. The bigger idiot I am the more perfect my impersonation of myself. I am "Big Daddy"—I am "Grando."

And I didn't fail on this trip. She has a new story to tell her husband, and I found again the panic of being two years old, which is a fear that lives on in my body—nothing I can do about it.

I've tried, believe me. I have been re-birthed, re-Rolfed, walked on red-hot coals—the works. (And nothing works.) I have had therapists who killed themselves while I was worrying about dying.

So, I release myself—and from my promise. ❖

"Navarro Beach Rock," Janet Ashford

In This Place

BY JEWELS MARCUS

In this place
Tambourines sink
Into black holes

Scarves can choke
The love right
Out of you

Dragonflies will
Courageously
Battle daisies

While that ruby of a future
Strides like starfish
Past the bog of fear

In this place
Hummingbirds fly rings
Around questions

Fiction

Hush

by Gloria Jorgensen

HUSH! *DON'T CRY NOW. Try to think of something else.* Any other day me and Wes'd be down to the creek fishing. There's a big ol' speckledy cat keep slipping down into his mud hole, evading our hooks. Thinks he's too clever for us, his wide flat mouth opening and closing slow, whiskers swaying, look like a Chinaman, bugged eyes staring out from two sides of that enormous head. Reckon how old he must be? I can nearly feel the sun on my back and hear them gulls calling overhead, feel Wesley's sweet curls cradling in the crook of my arm as we set there keeping still, trying to outsmart that cat. Them old-timers is wise. They seen a lot.

This here bench is worn smooth as a church pew. It's a shiny dark brown wood with dull places where people worried at the arm rests with sweaty palms, waiting for a man to tell them how their life was gonna turn out. There oughta be teeth marks.

The floor is cold white marble like tomb stones shot through with crazy grey lines running ever which a way. I hear deep voices coming and hard shoes clicking on the stair steps made saddle-shape by generations of people trudging up here. Things echo so with these high ceilings it sounds like a parade.

Jewel stops right slap in front of me and I'm staring square at his belt buckle. He's a big man; over six foot with a gut on him now, since I been feeding him so good all these years. Even his best suit coat and pleated pants can't hide that belly.

He says, "Charlotte." Loud. But I don't meet his gaze.

Then, louder, it's, "Lotti, look here at me."

"Don't call me Lotti," I tell him looking down and smoothing my flowered dress.

"It's just a pet name."

"I'm not your pet, Jewel."

"Don't get smart-mouth with me, girl."

"I'm not a girl either, I'm a grown woman."

"Listen at you. You best remember your place, missy. You're still ignorant even if you did read a few issues of *Psychology Today* in some lady-doctor's office."

"Maybe, J. W., but I'm not stupid. I figured that out."

"And look where it's got you. No man's ever gonna look at you twicet, say nothing about marrying you. It doesn't look like your lawyer's bothered to show either. You're going to need all the friends you can get, so you'd best play nice."

He turns on his heel, leaving me shut-mouthed and frozen like a startled doe.

I purely hate that sorry sum-bitch. Jesus said it's a sin to hate but he wasn't never married. It makes a difference.

Jewel never did want to talk to me in the first place. He just wanted to make a show of looking like we was talking. Then he'd imagine everybody was saying, "Why look there at Jewel Hightower. His wife's divorcing him but he still went over to her for a friendly chat. Isn't he a fine fellow?"

He's got a streak of good ole' boy in him the size of a double-wide trailer house. If he'd a been a Roman soldier nailing Jesus Christ hisself to the cross, Jewel woulda stopped and shot the breeze with Him whilst he was a hammering. I can't stand that, hail-fellow-well-met nonsense. It's like trying to hold a conversation with Saran Wrap.

I been trying to get a holt of my lawyer, Mr. Laude, for three days running. He won't return my calls. Yesterday I sat in his waiting room from the minute they opened until they locked the door behind me. He never did show his face. I know for a fact he talked to his secretary several times. He never would talk to me, though. I'm so scared I can hardly breathe. Why would he do that?

There's a young black woman sitting way down at the other end of the bench. Her skin glistens a beautiful blue-black like you don't hardly never see no more. I could look at her all day, her features are so thick and pronounced. She has two toddlers, chocolate brown color, and a baby who's fussing.

"Need some help?" I ask, catching her eye by practically laying on the floor to get into her line of vision.

"Nah, I be all right."

I scoot down to her end of the bench anyway to ease the loneliness.

"Get back here, Virgil." She says, grabbing at one of the toddlers, but he gets away.

"Here. Let me hold the baby." I reach for the pink bundle.

I'm never sure what to say to black people. I want to be friendly, same as with white folks, but I worry they'll hate me just for being white. Not that I'd blame them. Babies are different. They don't know what color they are yet, or what color I am.

"Are all these kids yours?" I ask. She don't look like she's but about eighteen herself.

"Yeah. They mine. They fixing to be all mine."

"You're getting divorced today, too?"

"What else you think I be here for?" She sounds disgusted with me for being so simple-minded. Virgil squirms and she smacks him on the leg saying, "Keep still, boy, 'fore I go outside and pick me a switch." He commences wailing and buries his head in her lap.

"Is your husband letting you keep them?" I sway back and forth with the baby who puts her fingers in my mouth.

"Letting me?" She sniffs. "I don't even know where he at. I'm just divorcin' his sorry ass to get out from under his bills."

"I wish my husband would run off and leave me and Wesley alone."

"You got kids?" She asks, stroking Virgil now. Soothing him.

"Just one," I tell her.

"Your husband want it?"

"He's fighting me for him, but I don't believe he wants him. He just doesn't want me to have him."

"You lucky, girl. Let him have the kid."

"No. I couldn't stand being away from my son like that. I'd as soon lose a leg." I rock the baby, feeling her breath on my neck. It's just about the sweetest thing in the world. When Wesley was a baby we'd sit and rock for hours. His breathing set my pace, kept me anchored in time.

Seems like lately I've kinda started to drift, like I was doing when Jewel put me in that mental hospital. Time slips around me. I get lost. I wasn't that sick then. I was just afraid I might could do something if I didn't get away from Jewel telling me how to be all the time.

The baby jumps. "Rabbit run over her grave," her mama says.

"She's just dreaming." I could hold her like this forever. Maybe I'd lose my mind if somebody took her away when I wasn't ready. I lean my face down and stroke my cheek across her soft, fine, curly hair. Then I give her back to her mama. I don't want to go crazy.

There's a big open sash window facing east and I go over to see if Mr. Laude's car is parked in front of the white clapboard house they turned into his office. It's something to do, an excuse to look at the live oaks dripping with Spanish moss and the palm trees growing in the courthouse square. My lawyer isn't coming. I know that. What I don't know is why.

Hot air from outside hits me like a blast from a gas space heater when you first light it. I can smell the pulp mill from here, all sulfur-ish and rotten like the fires of hell. Jewel comes home stinking of it everyday, even though he's got a desk job, management. He's a showboat.

We haven't lived here long. J. W. made the decision to take this job by himself. Then he packed up me and Wesley with the furniture and here we are. South Georgia, flat, hot and humid. My friends, my family, everything I knew, all left behind like yesterday's trash.

When we arrived with the U-Haul, Jewel says, "Look at it, Lotti. This is where we'll spend the rest of our lives." It made me feel so tired. I don't want to know what I'm going to be looking at every day from now on, even if some of it is considered to be a resort. Men in plaid pants chasing little white balls with sticks. God in Heaven help me. And yachts, oh, Lord. There's too many places I haven't seen; places I've read about and heard of all over the world. I want to travel and be broad, but that minute I knew it would never happen. I felt a door slam shut right in my face.

I try to pray, but God's a man, too. There's no way He could understand how I feel.

I have a dream that comes back again and again. Something huge and heavy is rolling toward me. I know it will crush me. My hand touches something soft at the same instant it feels a blade, cold, hard, sharp. I don't know what to pay attention to. It terrifies me more than dying. I have always dreamed this dream. I can't run, scream or cry. That's how I feel now watching Jewel and his lawyer coming toward me.

"Lotti, you know Frank." Jewel says all friendly and butter wouldn't melt in his mouth.

"Morning, Mr. Brown." I say, like I was taught. Mama always said, difficult situations are no excuse for bad manners. Being rude shows a person is trash.

"Hello, Mrs. Hightower. It appears your Mr. Laude isn't planning on joining us today."

"Yes, I noticed that myself." I'm looking at the toe of my pumps.

"You'd save us all a lot of aggravation if we could just settle this out here among ourselves instead of taking up the judge's time."

"That wouldn't be legal, would it?" I ask.

"Oh, it would be legal alright. I'd see to that." He grins.

"Well, it don't sound like too good of a idea to me. I think I'll just wait on the judge seeing as how we've got this far."

"Suit yourself, but he does not like for people to waste his time."

"Come on, Lotti, be reasonable." Jewel says, sticking his nose right slap in the middle of my business. "What do you expect the judge to do?"

"From what I been told," I says, "no man is ever got custody of a child in the state of Georgia, ever. I don't expect some little old judge down in Glynn County is gonna be the first one to do that when we all know that I ain't done nothing wrong. I reckon I expect that judge to make sure things are fair."

"Fair." Jewel snorts. "You think he's gonna take up for you like Perry Mason? You're just not practical. You never have learned to live in the real world."

When I was little there was a sampler in the sewing room. It said, "A STITCH IN TIME SAVES NINE." I thought it was a riddle. How could you take a stitch in time? What nine would you save? Was it like the Little Shoemaker? "SEVEN WITH ONE BLOW." That was flies. Or, "TIME FLYS LIKE AN ARROW BUT FRUIT FLIES LIKE A BANANA." No, that was a joke.

I wish I could take a stitch in time now, make a tuck, save two, me and Wesley. Or we could fly out of this time, fly like an arrow, out of this place where men decide everything. Wes will be a man one day. If only I can have a hand in his raising up, he might can be the sort of man who remembers his heart.

A door bangs open so loud I nearly 'bout jump out of my skin. A woman using her outside voice says, "Hightower versus Hightower" which is us, but she's just saying words, not really calling people.

Jewel and Mr. Brown gesture for me to go in first like gentlemen. It frightens me having them at my back. Seems like every time they mention my lawyer not being around they get these smirky looks on their faces. They don't seem quite as surprised by the whole thing as I am.

I'm expecting to walk into a big echoing courtroom, but this is small. The walls are lined with books so perfect they don't look real, but I can smell the leather and the scent of lemon Pledge. Somebody must've just polished that big cherry wood desk. It shines like a dark mirror.

There's a window pulled shut to keep the judge's air conditioning in. This room has low ceilings and plush carpeting. It must be chambers. We're told to sit. The lady who called us in doesn't stay. I don't see no court reporter or nobody like that. It's just us three and the judge setting behind that enormous desk. Maybe he'll say we have to come back some day when Mr. Laude can make it. I was ready for this to be over and done with, it's dragged on so long. But not like this. I hope they can't see how bad I'm shaking. I must look like I've got the palsy.

The judge is white-headed, stout and old. He sure looks like he should be wise by now, a grandfatherly figure, someone who will know my predicament and look after me. He'll be like Solomon and see that I am the real one to mother Wes because I'll give my son up before I'll let him be tore in half.

He looks at me and says, "Are you Mrs. Hightower?"

"Yes, Sir." I tremble.

"And you want a divorce?" He booms.

"Well, Sir, my lawyer isn't here."

"But you do want a divorce." He says like he's talking to a child.

"Well, Sir, I suppose—"

"Then we shall proceed." He turns his back on me.

The judge and Mr. Brown start talking. A lot of it I can't follow. I hear the judge ask, "And Mrs. Hightower does not currently have steady employment?" His voice is dark and slow, like sorghum syrup.

"That is correct." Mr. Brown says, like he knows all about me.

I can't help speaking up. "But, your Honor, Jewel told me to quit my regular job and take Wesley to Atlanta where my people can help us out. And he promised if I did that he wouldn't fight me for custody so I—"

Judge Moseley shifts his eyes lazily my way, like an old alligator laying in the sun. Seems like he forgot I was in the room. The thick sugary voice says, "Honey, it's not your turn to talk right now. You have to wait your turn."

It takes every ounce of gumption I've got to answer back. "Yes, Sir, but he's making it sound like I'm lazy and I'm not; I been cleaning folks houses and giving tours of the islands and the Okefenokee and learning Gulla and Geechee, and weaving baskets from the marsh grasses, and working hard to take care of Wesley. Ask that Social Worker Lady. Wesley told her he wants to stay with me."

"I'm sure you are a very good girl." He drawls through thick slack lips, gazing directly at my chest, then down at my lap and back up again. "But this is a legal proceeding and we have certain rules. Now, do not interrupt us again or I may have to have you removed. Can you understand what I'm telling you?"

I do understand. There is no help for me in this room. There never was. I am trying not to cry. If I start, it may become a scream and I am afraid I'll never be able to stop. These men will say I'm unstable, not fit. They will not equate it with a mother's grief over loss. It seems my only prayer is to sit still and behave, like always.

It's over. The judge says Wesley will live with his daddy and I can see him all I want, as long as me and Jewel agree. We can't agree on the day's headlines. I sit there, trying not to make a scene. J. W. is still in charge of everything. I have to figure out how to live in this place I can't afford.

Outside I blink in the brightness. There's a white hole burned in the sky.

Things pull loose inside me as I try to walk, like a fish being gutted when it's not dead. The fish I was has to die now, mouth opening, closing, gasping, trying to learn to breathe air on land. Turn loose of the

57

life you've known, fish. Take your spirit to heaven. Tell King Solomon this is a new time with judges who are no longer wise. Who will protect the children? A fish isn't strong enough. The glaring sun feels like it's bleaching something out of me.

I find my old car, wrench the door open with a screech, roll down windows I can reach and begin to sob. But the heat catches up with me and so does the stench from the pulp mill, so I crank her up. I'm not going to die with that fish.

My car moves majestically like a float in a parade. On the way to the island, marsh grasses stretch lush and green, and shrimp boats making their way along inland rivers seem to be sailing through a flat, endless prairie. Sea gulls swoop and dive around the trailing nets like bridesmaids in attendance.

Now I know it is time to be a bird—not a caged bird, a yard bird, or even a sea gull. It's time for me to become an eagle. ❖

Non-Fiction

Excerpt from *Standing in Gorda*

by Tony Camarda

2001.09.14, 11:20 a.m., Elk, California

WOKE UP AT 4 A.M. TODAY. Time to go. Mendocino County feels like an island in a different universe. After hitchhiking 800 miles into the end of the world, it has been a most welcome and needed sanctuary. But continue. Go! Get back on the road. See more. Thoughts of carving a small, invisible niche in Mendo are premature at best. The show goes on. San Francisco and Los Angeles still to come. If Godzilla attacks those cities, I will be there to see it.

Feeling oddly guilty about not being in New York right now. Pictures on the Internet, words on NPR, amidst this ocean fog mountain wonderland—I don't entirely feel it. I've become like those people I saw on the bus the day-of. It's not quite real. And I was there a week and a half ago. When I worked construction down there two years ago, not a day went by when I wouldn't morbidly visualize them toppling over. A certain tingle from imagining the inconceivable. And it happened. Though they didn't topple. Strange.

Walked down Albion Ridge to Highway 1 at about 9 A.M.

Feeling good. Hyper. Inertia returning.

Fifteen minute wait. Minivan, new. In broken, fractured English my patron tells me he is going all the way to San Francisco. No way. I can make it in one ride! He's going inland, on scenic 128, and taking 101 South the last 80 miles. Hmmmm. That's against the rules. I'm supposed to stay on the coast. Must think fast. I get in.

Jose lives in Oakland. Hispanic in some way. Carpenter. Asks if I know about Jesus. Yes, yes. A perfectly nice, safe man. Not too much English.

Three miles later we reach the spot where Highway 1 merges with 128 East. To continue on the Pacific Coast Highway you have to turn right over the Navarro River Bridge. I communicate to Jose that I want to get off at the bridge. He seems concerned at first, mentions something about Jesus, but pulls over. I thank him and watch the silver minivan plunge inland and disappear around a bend, soon to be engulfed in a canopy of big redwoods.

I walk to the middle of the bridge. It is late summer, and the Navarro River is running low. It doesn't rain here from June to September. A faraway clatter resounds off the river canyon walls. At first its origin is uncertain. As it comes closer I recognize it as the sound of a blender having a heart attack. The beat-up pickup makes the river turn from Albion and I see the driver. This is the same mold of older gentleman who has given me numerous rides. I'm not hitching at this moment, just loitering halfway across the bridge watching the river flow, but the truck squeaks and clunks to a stop. Over the retching din my patron offers:

"Going to Elk."

Elk is the next town, five miles down. I hop in. No names, no explanation. Pleasant small talk about the weather. My patron mentions, with almost cheerful surprise, "Muffler took a crap today."

We climb in elevation. This stretch of coast is remote. My patron drives slowly. Absolutely no hurry. As we pass cars coming in the other direction, the gentleman bends his left hand off the steering wheel in a two-and-a-half-fingered salute. He does it for everybody. There is something terribly endearing about this. He *is* this place, calmly meandering down this beautiful road on a Friday morning. I am struck with the strongest desire to be 60 years old, driving a clunky Toyota to my general store, waving at everybody.

At the south end of Elk the road does some serious switchbacks downhill. Cars have to go slow, which is good for me. Not really any good shoulders, which is bad. I stand for about 45 minutes with little traffic and no luck. I walk downstream about a quarter mile and find a decent spot, but I've been here almost an hour.

I'd be almost to Marin if I had stayed with Jose. But that is okay. I'm told that the coastline just gets more beautiful down towards Sonoma, though I don't see how that is possible.

2:15 P.M., JENNER, CA

I stand at the edge of Elk for two and a half hours. Finally picked up by a good-natured older man driving a huge Impala. Early '70s car. Get the impression that he might have bought it new. Irwin is his name. Irwin used to live around here, but now he lives in Louisiana, came out to the Bay Area to visit his son, rolled up to Mendo to visit the ghosts.

Irwin asks me if I am in College. Huh? I do look younger than twenty-eight, but I'm pretty sure I don't look quite that young. Maybe at 60 everyone in their twenties looks alike. He's telling me his youth-on-adventure stories soon enough.

"Hitchhiking used to be so easy. So easy. And not just out here. Everywhere. And not just in America. Everywhere. The whole world used to be so much more friendly. In '68 we were traveling across Europe, me and a few buddies, we'd made our way to Spain. Well, first, we're in Germany and we decide to rent a van. The trains, eh, you get from city to city on the trains. But if you want to travel Europe and actually see anything, meet real people, you have to drive yourself. This was all so much easier, and cheaper back then. And then—we've made it to the south of Spain. And by this time we'd picked up these girls, also just traveling, two Americans and a French girl, and we all decide that we should drive to Afghanistan …"

Irwin pauses here, aware of the fact that he needs to let that last fact sink in. Afghanistan. Yes, things have changed.

"And that drive—ferry across to Morocco, blazing through the

Sahara, just, ballin' in the moonlight in the desert, just …"

Irwin pauses here as well. Don't think it is for effect, though. Reliving "ballin' in the moonlight." Sounds like a good deal. He skips ahead to the part about entering Afghanistan.

"So we're smoking all this German hash all the way across the continent, two continents, wait, three! Four if you count the Middle East. Not thinking about anything at this point. Egypt, Iran, all of it is all good. People are just so nice in the Middle East. That's the thing that people don't understand about this bullshit in the media right now. Those people—I'd trust those people over modern-day Americans any day. Though—I don't know. Maybe things have changed over there, too. I don't know …"

Irwin stops the narrative again. Contemplating recent events. Sixty years of observing humanity. Ephemeral nature of it all. Really amazing how big this car is. There's at least five feet of empty space between Irwin and me.

The silence extends beyond my own mind's meandering and I need to know what happened in Afghanistan.

"Well what happened?"

"Oh. So we get to the border and the border, it's not some elaborate thing. It is a shack in the middle of nowhere. There's one guy. He's not wearing a uniform, at least, it didn't look like a uniform. Just, here's Iran, here's Afghanistan, here's the shack. And he's looking at our passports, speaks pretty good English, friendly, really fascinated to hear about all these places that we have been, and the brick of hash is just sitting there on the back seat, and he sees it, and suddenly he is like 'What is this?' And he grabs it, grabs the hash, and again he is saying, 'What is *this*? What is this shit?' And we're just crapping in our trousers. He walks back to the shack with our brick of hash, and I don't know is he on some radio, are we about to get disappeared to some Afghani prison forever, what is happening? No idea. The girls start crying. We're trying to shoosh them. Don't know why. I wanted to cry, too.

And this is all in maybe 40 seconds. A minute later the border guard is back, huge smile on his face, and he hands me the biggest brick of hash I have ever seen. A different brick. And he says, 'This is the good shit. You come to Afghanistan you smoke Afghani. Not that European shit. This is the good shit. Enjoy your stay in Afghanistan.'"

Irwin is laughing. I'm laughing, too. Irwin stops laughing soon and he seems melancholy. I feel it, too. That was the world when he was a young man. That is not the world anymore. Well maybe there is a border guard somewhere on this planet who will hand you a brick of hashish in 2001. Maybe. And maybe the stories I will tell of this trip in 33 years will blow the mind of the young hitchhiker I pick up in my flying nuclear car on the moon.

6:30 P.M., Mill Valley, California

The Sonoma coast is in fact, the most beautiful stretch of coastline I've seen thus far. Not really sure how to quantify/qualify that. You could make the case that endless expanse of ocean all looks alike. And also that the topography of the Western US coastline is a generally similar arrangement of rock and tree and dirt. Sunlight is about the same. Fragrant ion-infused air, about the same. This is all true.

Maybe what makes the Sonoma coast so stunningly fantastic is the almost complete lack of human monkeys and their buildings. The south end of Mendocino County is a little town called Gualala. The "G" is pronounced like a "W", so it is Wa-la-la. We pass into Sonoma County and in the 40 miles to Jenner don't see another town, another coastal resort, nothing. There is a historic site called Fort Ross, that's it. And most of the drive takes place at least 200 feet in elevation, on the narrowest of twisty roads, just a slash cut into the steep cliff-side, turkey vultures gliding high. How did they ever build this road?

At Jenner the coastal highway is again at sea level, and slightly inland. Well not quite inland, but upriver. The Russian River meets ocean here, and the teeny town of Jenner is just east of the spot where the mouth of the river yawns wide and snakes slowly to the sea. The view from the highway is of marshy little islands populated by easy birds.

South of the town is a road that twists up into the hills. This road goes all the way to Santa Rosa and the main vein. This is Irwin's route. He stops at the Jenner gas station to top off his ancient behemoth. We part with a good word. I get to walking. Hitching out of the gas station is a maybe, but legs need a little action. The river is humid and low. Irwin passes me on the way to the turn-off and gives a little honk and wave. He stops. Pulls over. I get to the window.

"Here you go, got a cooler of them."

He is offering me a nice cold plastic bottle of water. Thank you much. And he's off.

About a quarter mile of walking, maybe more. I get to the "T" where Irwin rolled up inland. Good wide shoulder. Soft gravel. Coming from the North the road is a tight turn a 100 yards upstream so traffic won't be at full speed by the time they see me. And good position to solicit patrons coming from the East. Not many of those.

Probably two hours at this nice spot. It is a Honda Accord station wagon that finally stops, coming from the North. Bicycles on the back. White paint and dusty, Massachusetts plates. A couple. Mid-twenties. The girl is driving. Fella asks me: "Where 'ya headed?"

"I'm trying to get to Mill Valley, in Marin."

The couple confers for just a moment and he says: "Yeah, we could get you there. We're going to the city, but we're going to cut across towards Petaluma to go to Whole Foods. Then hit the 101."

I have a moment of pause here. I want to tell them that there is a Whole Foods literally two blocks from where I am going. Where they are going to cut inland is maybe 30 miles north of Mill Valley, which means I'll miss the chance to hitch the most remote stretch of Marin County coastline, and the challenge of getting into Mill Valley through the back door, over Mt. Tamalpais. I'm thinking all this in about 1.5 seconds. I'm not supposed to hitch anywhere but the coast, can't even cheat for 30 miles. But I've been standing here for two hours. And this couple seems nice and I think they are offering to drop me off exactly where I am going. I calculate this last bit in .75 seconds. I get in the car.

There is a sliver of space to sit in the back. They have clearly been doing some serious traveling and the station wagon is packed. The car smells like oranges. This is confirmed by the fella' offering me an orange in the first minute. Thank you much.

His name is Phil. Hers is Heather. She is pretty and earthy, long black hair, comfortable clothes, seems grounded. I can't see Phil too well because I'm sitting right behind him. I know he is clean cut, wears glasses, also an easy disposition and grounded.

They ask for my story and I tell them.

Heather wants to know if any women have picked me up driving alone. Yeah, there was that one the first day. Is that the only one? Almost had a blind date at the fish shack, that was sort of a pickup. No, no other women. Wait! How could I forget?! Those two women, back to back, who got me to Bandon. And the corn dog eater who dropped me off near the cheese factory. Huh, the world ends, I hide in the woods for three days and I almost forget everything.

We come to a complete stop due to cows in the road. Steep hillside to the left. Steep hillside to the right. No sign of a ranch anywhere.

Heather and Phil tell me that this adventure is a whirly-do around America seeing friends and family before they spend two years in Antarctica. They've been accepted by a government program that hires intelligent young adventurers to do the jobs that make the scientists feel like they are living in a town. Movie theatre ticket-taker. Barista. Bowling alley shoe disinfector. That sort of thing. It pays well, sort of. And housing is, of course, taken care of. And they get ample time off to explore the landscape, led by professional guides. There's only a few months out of the year when that is possible, however.

"Are you worried that you might, you know, go insane?"

Heather answers this: "They provide psychological counseling to deal with the cabin fever. And it's not like we're trapped. If we're there a few months and it is totally awful we can come back. I hope we make it at least a year, though. We agreed to make it at least six months and then commit to another six months. Two years is scary, to think about two years doing anything. We just want to get there and make the best of it."

Well okay. She certainly sounds like she has convinced herself. Phil doesn't say too much on the subject. Interesting pair. They must really like each other to go to freakin' Antarctica together.

Wonder if I'll ever like anybody that much.

Well, probably.

The real question is whether any woman will like/tolerate me that much, let's be honest here.

I ask them if the program looks for people with a specific educational background. Not really, Heather says: "Well, the application process is really in-depth. All these background checks and FBI stuff. But no, you just have to have a degree. And be willing to do it. I was a Marine Biology major."

"And I studied Comparative Literature," Phil offers.

"I think they want people who are smart, but not too smart."

"Yeah," I say, "that sounds like most employers."

Heather: "Exactly. So we figure we might as well do that in Antarctica." ❖

Non-Fiction

Rip Van Winkle and Me

by Aron Lee Bowe

MOURNING DOVES WERE PILE-DRIVING a rusty spike into my brain with their damn cooing. Blasted birds! Stupid to drink four glasses of wine last night. One was more than enough to give me a splitting headache. This Napa Valley hangover wasn't a hell-of-a-lot different from one induced by a fine Ohio brew, or maybe I was homesick? No, that's not right. Muddled is a more apt description.

My eyeballs made their usual squishy sound as I rubbed, like chew toys attacked by angry poodles. I blinked a few times and tried to focus on my bedroom walls. Green to blue to purple to pink to yellow and back again. Though none of my new house mates liked my rainbow paint job, I had saved a bundle by buying the rejects from the Sherwin Williams Paint Store. They practically gave the paint away for two dollars a can. The colors were similar to those of a cake I once baked for a birthday party, and no one—*besides me*—wanted to eat.

Why were people so narrow-minded? What was the big deal? Hadn't we all read *Green Eggs and Ham?*

Out of whack, that's what I am. I am out of whack. No one but me wanted to eat a green egg or, for that matter, a dazzling green and blue marbled sponge cake with rainbow marshmallow frosting. I let out a deep self-pitying moan.

With a mighty stretch I reached for my diary on the cinder block bookcase. The floor was covered in a thin white layer of flea powder, and I didn't want to contaminate my semi-clean paisley sheets with poison. My drawing pencil fell, but I wasn't up for retrieving it from under the bed for fear of vomiting.

As I reclined on my feather pillow, something pawed outside my door. "Go away, Nimrod!" I yelled and gingerly leaned sideways to grab a slipper. Though my aim was right on, the slipper made only a muffled thump as it hit the vivid pink door.

Nimrod, with his super-dog hearing, gave a little whine of protest. The damn fleabag!

Unfortunately for my poor flea-bitten skin, the warm sunlight of my upstairs bedroom attracted the household's menagerie. It was the only warm room in the house, since my broke house mates and I opted to go without heat this winter. For some damn reason, I was the only human in our house tormented by the small wingless jumping blood-suckers from hell.

I opened page one of my diary and read my New Year's resolutions. One: work towards more self-discipline and self-motivation. Two: be less of a lazy individual.

"Right," I muttered. "As soon as I finish my nap." Maybe I'll stay in bed today. What's the point of getting up? It wasn't as if I had a job—or friends—or a boyfriend. I frowned and scratched two of my infected bites.

My mother's nagging words filled my brain. "Aron, you're making a terrible mistake. He'll leave you, then what will you do?" Her round face flushed hot fury into her threat. "If you go to Mexico with that dirty hippy, you're sure as hell not coming back home. Stay in Ohio, and we'll set you up in a nice apartment and buy you all the clothes you need to get a good teaching job at a local high school." Her voiced dripped honey with her pecuniary bribe, but her eyes were squinty blue ice.

God, I'm so pathetic. Even in my imagination, I was incapable of responding with a single word in my defense. Was I born without a backbone? I am out of whack.

The house cat meowed and scratched the door. "Forget it, Tid-dlywink," I yelled. "You and your disgusting fur-balls are banned from this room. That goes for your fuzzy little sidekicks, too."

The huge black cat loved to sleep on my bed and the new calico kittens followed, even though he hissed and arched his back like a freaked out Halloween cat. Tiddlywink also spat at the two dogs, but Nimrod and Oscar paid no attention to the grumpy feline. The stinky mutts liked to snooze in the sunny spot on my braided rug. It was no wonder my legs were polka-dotted with bites from their damn flea circus.

My eyes gazed up at the white ceiling. Though I'd debated painting it deep blue with silver phosphorescent stars depicting the zodiac, I was glad that I hadn't. The ceiling was the blank canvas of my room, a Zen place for my mind. I stared—as if in a trance—and my eyes felt heavy. I couldn't shake the odd feeling that I'd fallen through a time-warp, or been asleep for ages like old Rip Van Winkle.

Moving a zillion miles from home without a single friend or acquaintance left me a bit shaken, as did having my parents disown me. But my mother's bribe was a sticky web that could suffocate my soul. Contrary to her dire prediction, I was the one to break up with the dirty hippy.

This peculiar sensation of time moving on without me wasn't merely my family melodrama, or the culture shock of coming back into the United States after living in Mexico. Simply moving to California from rural Ohio seemed to erase years from my age.

Every time I opened my mouth, my five house mates made me feel utterly naive and immature. Everyone I met in California seemed to have done it all and to be freer in both body and mind. The smallest things my house mates did amazed me.

Carlos cooked tortillas without a pan over the stove's gas flame. Yoshi bought fresh fish from the wharf and ate it raw. Barbara walked around the house completely naked—even during her periods. Ed claimed drugs were passé, and that I'd missed a hell of a decade. Rick informed me that he had scabies, a contagious skin disease that caused intense itching between his fingers, underarms, elbows, and genitals. He picked up the itch mite from one of his many girlfriends. This new contagion was not exactly a selling point for his free-love concept. Furthermore, what in the world were Carlos' two extremely handsome male friends from San Francisco doing together in his bedroom? It sure didn't sound like they were discussing sports.

Yep, I am totally out of whack. I sighed and scratched the inflamed red bite on the top of my big toe. Maybe I could buy flea collars for my ankles. Finally, a reason to get out of bed. Furthermore my throbbing head needed black coffee and my growling stomach wouldn't mind one of those hot corn tortillas with a dollop of Carlos' refried beans.

"Forget it, Mom," I said aloud. "I'm not using a frying pan." I bounced off my mattress, threw open the door, and didn't stop the animals stampeding past me into the warm light. ❖

"Foggy June Headlands," Janet Ashford

Fiction

Folie Beaujon

Excerpt from a novel, *The Appassionata* by Molly Dwyer

THÉODORE GÉRICAULT RAN HIS HAND over his stubbled head, feeling the unfamiliar sensation of shaved skin. The reflection staring back at him in the mirror was unrecognizable—gaunt cheekbones and sunken, predatory eyes reminiscent of a bird of prey. Falcon eyes, Jamar called them. The man he'd been, with his cryptic wit and pretty face, the man-about-town whom women turned to admire, had vanished even before the blade cut away the honeyed locks that graced his collar.

What had happened to the young gallant who wrapped his hair in paper curlers to heighten its bounce? Allié would be dismayed by the transformation, could she see it. Eugène had seemed close to tears last week. No one could fathom why Géricault had installed himself in a derelict studio on the abandoned parklands of Folie Beaujon at the western edge of Paris. He'd taken Jamar with him. The Arab played servant, student, and model as needed, a comforting chameleon, who spoke little and remained unflinchingly loyal. As for the location, the Beaujon hospital, a modest facility with a morgue, stood just around the corner. Géricault's dark descent had begun amongst its cadavers and he'd kept his vigil until nothing repelled him.

He contemplated his reflection. He hadn't slept in days, hadn't even tried, lying down last night in the same clothing he'd worn all week, clothing that smelled of cloying decay. The stink had ripened overnight and bordered on emetic. Grateful for the jug of water Jamar fetched, Géricault dipped his hands into the basin and brought the cool refreshment to his face.

It did little, however, for the apprehension that plagued his body. He had heard the rumblings over a week ago: His son—yes, he had a son—his son had been born without incident and delivered into the hands of a nursemaid who secreted the boy away. But no one had heard a word since. Géricault felt certain something had gone awry. The only trace of Hippolyte's existence was a birth record filed in Paris.

The painter frowned. He should have taken Allié and run off to Italy when he had the chance. His only victory lay in his son's name. The midwife had managed that much: Georges after Géricault's father; and Hippolyte—Greek for "I release the horses." Hippolyte, the wronged son of Theseus.

He wrapped his head in a paint-spattered rag and descended to the ground floor, pulling a kerchief from his pocket as he walked. He tied it tight over his nose, giving him the look of a finely wrought highwayman. It did nothing to alleviate the stench, and he gagged as he pushed open his studio door.

Pristine light glowed across the floor. Sketches covered his worktable, interspersed with the flush of color: bodies in various postures of repose and decay, studies of a raft and of the sea. Most of his efforts were small and fleeting, spiked at various intersections by larger pieces, six, even seven feet high.

Across the back wall he'd built a wooden frame. It took up the entire space, measuring over 16 feet tall and 23 feet wide. He'd stretched canvas to cover it and built a scaffolding in front, reaching its entire height. Mobile, he could push it along and work wherever he chose. It had been weeks in the making, as had the model that took up most of the floor: a raft, constructed with such accuracy that even the gaps between the planks replicated the original.

The flagship *Medusa* had carried 400 passengers, 160 crew members, and six lifeboats. One-hundred-fifty people had been cast adrift on a quickly constructed raft. After 13 days, only 15 remained, parched and fading.

Géricault approached his worktable and thumbed through a pile of sketches: impressions of men herded onto the makeshift barge; survivors hailing an approaching frigate; studies of the wind-filled sail; and a hell-like rebellion consciously reminiscent of Michelangelo. He pushed through the images quickly, looking for the head he'd painted of Jamar. Its radiance interested him. He'd imitated Caravaggio—manipulating light to achieve volume, to lift the figure off the page in three-dimensional relief. The draft gave Jamar a godlike quality. Now he combed over the picture as if someone else created it, and indeed he barely remembered the effort, so lost he'd been in the labyrinth of death.

"With the brush we merely tint," he mused, his kerchief muffling his words. "The imagination alone produces color." He held the painting up, then, overcome by an odor bordering on the macabre, he let it drop and pressed his hand against his nose, surveying the studio. Amputated body parts, whole arms and legs glared from among his sketches. They despoiled the raft, festering where they lay. They crept toward him like an opposing army arrayed for battle. He'd been collecting them, using them to create specific studies, then abandoning them one by one—like his son.

"My son," he whispered. "What has become of my son?"

He glanced toward the door half-expecting Jamal or Delacroix to burst in with news. What was it Michelangelo had said? *Genius is eternal patience.* Géricault let his gaze fall on a bloodied cloth that lay draped round a bulging prize he secured only last night. The sight sent a shiver across his shoulders. He stepped back, giving the thing wide berth, and turned his attention to one of the newspaper reports that lay scattered on the table. It was dated July 1816. What had he been doing two years ago? Studying art in Italy? Yes. And missing Allié so much that things had already come undone.

He passed over several handwritten accounts—he'd taken survivors' stories down, verbatim—and picked up a newly published book, *The*

Shipwreck. It lay open to the last page he'd studied and a passage circled in red paint. The moment he intended to portray. *The sight of this vessel spread among us a joy which it would be difficult to describe*, the red-painted words explained.

A fierce and articulate survivor, the author blamed the shipwreck on the Bourbon dynasty, which had taken up the reins of government after Napoléon's fall. The *Medusa*, he contended, ran aground because its captain was an Ultra-Royalist with friends in high places. A prissy idiot, an officer of the *ancien régime* who hadn't sailed in over 20 years.

The *Medusa* had broken up on a sandbar 60 miles off the coast of Senegal. Any competent sailor, the book argued, could have avoided the outcome. Géricault turned a page. The ship captain had plotted against Napoléon, returning to France only after Waterloo. He embodied everything the Bonapartistes found repugnant. The exposé articulated the cost of corruption, the malfeasance of the monarchy, and the irony of its restoration.

Géricault had spent long hours interviewing the book's author, so much so that he, himself, could describe the raft's fate with the clarity of a survivor. Siding with Bonapartistes unnerved the painter. Politics was not his style. He'd always found the propaganda in David's art distasteful.

"Passion matters. Truth. Obsession even—art for the sake of itself."

He set the book aside, restless, unable to work. "Not politics," he mumbled. Yet the politics of the shipwreck fit his mood. He wanted to disturb the complacency of the Académie. Everyone had fallen so easily back into supporting the monarchy. He wanted to cause a stir at next year's Salon. The undertaking was risky, elevating a distasteful controversy into a massive history painting, a gamble. And he had neither commission, nor reputation; he needed his work to sell.

Géricault surveyed the huge empty canvas that hung on the wall. Wasn't Diderot the one who spoke about that 'which stuns the soul'? Hadn't Diderot written about how the imprint of terror leads to the sublime? That's what Géricault wanted—to arouse terror, awe, and beauty simultaneously.

"Portray them the way they exist in nature, side-by-side."

He returned to the painting of Jamar's head. When he turned it upside down, the explicit use of light transformed the image into a blissful shepherd boy, Endymion, the moon pouring over his sleeping face. How remarkable that a shift in the viewpoint could change so much. And of course he would think of Endymion; Allié had christened him that when they first made love, casting herself as the goddess, Sélène.

"We shall meet forever in our dreams, *mon amour*."

Géricault felt a surge of loathing for his uncle. "Allié," he called out, "*Je t'aime. Je te désire.*" His words hung in the air as his hand crashed down on the tabletop. What madness. Would he ever see her again?

"Our earthly desires are but idle fancies." He muttered and, righting the painting, forced himself to study it. Jamar's neck bent back now, the face falling away. Still, the boy seemed too pretty for death.

Géricault set the painting down and tightened the kerchief against his face. He stood for a moment contemplating the bloody parcel on his worktable, then moved to disrobe it, but his nerve failed. He could not. He took up another sketch instead, a study that defined the shape of the composition. A large *x* stretched from bodies in the lower left, to a figure waving towards the distant horizon at the top. Géricault traced the second axis with his finger. It fell from a wind-filled sail, down to the lower right where the raft met the sea.

He returned to the passage he'd marked in the book. The moment of aroused promise. He read the words aloud. "*Fear, mixed with hope— but the raft commanded little elevation above the water. It remained indistinguishable at such a distance. They'd done what they could: piled up casks, fixed handkerchiefs to the top. In spite of their signals, the brig disappeared. They fell from delirium and joy into the pit of dejection.*"

That delicate threshold between life and death, that's what he sought. And it made sense that to paint such a moment he needed to understand it. Géricault looked again to the canvas, empty, but for his vision. He imagined the same shape moving from the lower left to the top, and from the upper left to the bottom. Like Michelangelo, his figures would loom larger than life. In his mind's eye, they already populated the painting.

He pulled up the one stool in his studio and sat, exhausted by his restless churning. His hand went to his thigh. Some days ago, it had developed a strange burning, a numbness that felt strange to the touch. It seemed to emanate from the hint of pain that lived in his spine. He refused to speak of it or even think of it. It would pass. He crossed his arms over the open pages of the book and buried his head. If only he could sleep. He closed his eyes, remembering the day he saw the Sistine Chapel for the first time. God, how he'd wept. What a feat. What an impossible feat the man had enacted. Michelangelo's images literally fell out of the sky. Perspective. Yes. It affected everything.

Géricault had thrown himself on the marble floor that day, on his back so he could gaze upward—until some poor monk reprimanded him for his lack of respect. One did not lie on the floor in God's house. Perhaps not, but certainly one must lie like that under Michelangelo's ceiling. Hadn't the artist himself done as much—the paint spattering in his eyes, blinding him? Twenty months and no one to grind his colors.

Genius is eternal patience.

One hundred and fifty people reduced to fifteen, and they'd eaten the flesh of the dead to survive. Géricault's head felt heavy. What was that in the distance? Ocean waves? Yes. They towered over him, lifting into the sky; they rose so high over the creaking raft, he feared they would consume him. And the sun, like some pagan god, burrowed into his flesh and drank his blood.

"*Mon Dieu,*" he whispered. "*Je meurs.*" I am dying.

Géricault awoke with a start, Michelangelo's ghost whispering in his ear, "*It is better to be afraid, than abandoned by God.*"

The painter jumped up. The sun had passed its zenith, and confused by the change in the light, he climbed the scaffolding to its top, pacing its length. The structure swayed, an unstable perch designed to move.

That's what he must paint, an unstable perch. The public must experience peril, be part of the horror, feel lost at sea. He had to create visceral proof of the abomination. One does not desist from brutality and callous indifference toward one's fellow without sharing in their panic and pain.

"Especially one with the wealth and power of Jean-Baptiste." Géricault growled his discontent. "Hippolyte." He called his son's name, and lifting an arm over his head, clenched his fist. "You who run with the horses. You who are born of my flesh. Hippolyte, I dedicate this to you."

He scrambled down the scaffolding and climbed onto the raft, skirting a decomposing limb, ignoring it, studying the empty canvas instead. The eye must travel of its own accord to the horizon: that line separating sea from sky. Onlookers must feel seized by the waves and threatened, must seek rescue as desperately as the men lost at sea. Yes. He would paint along the traditional axis, a history painting after David, but no shiny polish. A modern history. A deplorable history. No glorious Napoléon atop his windblown steed. No. Only the extraordinary tragedy of ordinary men.

What would the Salon say to that? Or the Painter of the Revolution? Would David repeat the words of astonishment he'd uttered about Géricault's, Officer on Horseback? Géricault had won gold at the 1812 Salon and again in 1814, and all David could say was, "Where did this come from? I do not recognize this brush." Jacques-Louis David, the unrivaled, the exiled. David believed only in the genius of his own students. *D'accord.* So be it. David would recognize Géricault's brush this time. They would all recognize Géricault's brush.

"It's not simply hope. I must portray the crushing blow of disappointment—the fact defeat drives us from one another."

Géricault returned to his worktable and let his falcon eyes rest on the bloody bundle, staring at it for some time before lifting both hands in reverence. He'd told himself for weeks, months even, that he must assemble a visual witness, must evoke with pigment *Medusa's* undoing.

His teachers complained that two painters warred within him. They said he applied his tones with a nervous hand, and must embrace either the neoclassicism of David or the *terribilità* of Michelangelo—that he could not wander between them. Géricault did not agree. The parlance meant nothing to him. The way his brush stroked the canvas—that's what mattered—a lover's touch gliding across living flesh. Allié had taught him that.

"Allié." He sang her name like a hymn while layering muslin over his kerchief so only his eyes showed through. He pulled on his gloves, leather, with the fingertips cut away. He was ready. He touched the bloodied cloth cautiously, unwrapping its cargo as if he handled a volatile explosive. Half his mind dwelt on the bundle, half crept off to Allié, imagining himself sneaking into La Chesnay and devouring her lovely smile, her laughter, her touch.

"*Tas de merde!*" The bloodied sheet fell away and he howled through gritted teeth. "You pile of shit."

Hardened by rigor mortis, the blackened head forced him back. Sunken eyes glared at him from a green-bloated face. He ripped off his gloves, yelling his disgust. "You whore. You son of a bitch." He stopped and stood, waiting. He'd learned if he did not resist, his sensory impulses dulled and accommodated the horror.

"The only thing certain in this world is pain."

He concentrated on a gleam of light falling through the window, on the way it created shadows, then grabbing his charcoal and a sketch pad, he worked the image onto paper, clinging to the patterns of light and dark—his raft in a hellish sea. One sketch followed another—dozens, changing his angle, his perspective, his point of focus—until he developed a strange sort of affection for the horrible thing. He took up his knife and pulled a bit of color to the center of his palette: Naples yellow. Caravaggio's favorite. He subdued it with a touch of ochre. Prussian blue drove a gray cast into the mix, a bead of white, then vermillion; pallid flesh, the jaundiced tones of death. He applied his color quickly, laying down the contours of decay, organizing his efforts around contrasts, moving from dark to light; the length and direction of each brush stroke expressing his purpose.

When he had exhausted himself, he set a sculpture pedestal next to his paint cabinet. The cupboard housed all his pigments and binders, everything he needed to paint. Inlaid with a design of light ash, it was the only piece of furniture he'd brought with him from his studio on Rue des Martyrs. It sat under the window opposite his canvas, and he positioned the pedestal next to it. He wanted to give the demon head a place of honor where it could watch him work. He pulled on his gloves again, clenched his teeth and shivered as he lifted the thing with his palms, his bare fingertips raised off its rotting flesh.

The eight feet from the table to the window loomed in front of him, the pedestal as distant as the farthest star. He crossed the expanse blindly, spittle dripping down his chin. As he set the head down, a loud pounding rattled the studio door, the shock of it taunting him, summoning madness.

"*Putain de merde!*" he cried out. "Go away!"

"Théo," Delacroix's familiar voice penetrated. "For God's sake man, open the door. I've news for you—about Allié." ❖

Non-Fiction

Piano, Piano

by Nona Smith

BY THE END OF THE SECOND WEEK of our three-week tour of Italy, my husband and I decide we need a vacation from our vacation. We plan a day completely to ourselves. Our traveling companions rise early to board a coach to Assisi, but we stay snuggled in bed, waking well after our hotel stops serving breakfast. We dress for the late spring weather of Tuscany and, arm in arm, stroll in the direction of our only commitment for the day, an 11:00 a.m. massage at the local spa. Our mantra is the Italian expression of the moment: *"piano, piano."* Loosely translated, it means take it easy, go the way the river flows.

Before long, we happen upon a small café with a sunny patio where we order *due cappuccini*, point to two calorie-ridden items in the pastry case, and take one of the tiny outside tables. We sip coffee in the sun, purr over the butter-laden apricot pastries and check our upper lips for steamed milk moustaches. We continue our walk to the spa. So far, the day is perfect.

We arrive at *Chianciano Spa Terme* with 15 minutes to spare. A concrete wall surrounds the facility and, when we enter the naturally flowing thermal spa, we see what we couldn't see from the outside: a square compound composed of low buildings facing a grassy open-air park. A bandstand is located at one end of the green with lawn chairs haphazardly facing it. A dozen people are seated casually, listening to classical music played by a young couple on cello and flute. We decide to come back to the music after our massages, but for now, we follow the smell of sulfa that guides us to the treatment center.

Opening the door of a dome-topped building marked *Spa*, we step into another world.

A crescent-shaped reception room, lit in soft shades of lavender and violet, flaunts a highly polished stainless steel counter. It echoes the shape of the room, and we forget that from the outside this is a rambling, narrow-windowed, cement building.

Behind the counter, two young, attractive receptionists are busy at work, one on the phone, the other assisting a couple attempting to make a credit card transaction. Both women are dressed in sleeveless sundresses that show off their tanned, toned arms. They wear jingling bangles on their wrists, and the gold rings on their fingers flash.

Three couples stand in line ahead of us. The credit card transaction is causing a delay, so I entertain myself by reading the posters on the wall. One (in Italian, French, English and German) is titled *Rules of Behavior in Chianciano Spa Terme*. It begins: *We wish everyone to have an enjoyable spa experience. Therefore, no smoking or loud talking inside the spa is permitted. Bathing caps must be worn in the swimming pool. Slippers (provided) must be worn at all times. Bathing suits must be worn during all spa treatments."*

I go back to Art who patiently stands in line. "We need bathing suits," I tell him. "Who says?"

I point to the sign. "It says so right there."

"That's ridiculous. You don't need a bathing suit to get a massage."

"Well, we do *here*. But we can wear our underwear, I guess."

I'm not really concerned about this wrinkle. *Piano, piano.*

But I am worried that the clock on the wall reads five minutes to 11:00, and we are no closer to the front of the line than when we arrived. Arriving late will impact our relaxing massage time, and I was looking forward to every minute of being kneaded and stretched.

I tap my foot in impatience. Art gently puts his foot on top of mine and I look down. What I see distracts me: Italian shoes. Earlier in the trip, I bet my traveling companions I could tell an Italian woman solely (no pun intended) by her shoes. Italian women do not wear tennis or *walking* shoes. They wear high fashion shoes, with spiky heels. I now have a chance to test my theory.

The woman directly in front of me is wearing a short, black dress, and *yes!* green leather, gladiator-looking shoes with straps that run halfway up her calf. They have five-inch heels. The woman in front of her perches on a high-heeled version of red and teal-colored saddle shoes. At the front of the line, I see dainty, black flats, decorated with tiny gold studs. Italian women, all; I'd bet a pasta dinner on it.

Since the line is still not moving, I direct my attention to an observation I'd been making about men's hair. I'd noticed that: *(one)* very young Italian males wear their hair in modified, product-laden Mohawks; *(two)* if an adult Italian male still has a full head of hair, he flaunts it, cutting it very short in back, and leaving it thick and wavy on top: and *(three)* Italian men do not do comb-overs. Men with fading follicles shave their heads smooth. Unlike Samson, this seems to restore their machismo. Two weeks in Italy and I've yet to see a single comb-over.

The couple at the front of the line, credit card issues at last resolved, moves down the counter. Each is handed a large plastic bag emblazoned with the spa's name, a pair of white flip-flops and locker keys. They disappear through a lavender and purple beaded curtain. The line inches forward. The clock reads 11:00 A.M. I resume my toe tapping.

The next pair proceed quickly through the registration and payment process, but the twosome directly in front of us wants to move their afternoon appointments to an earlier time. The receptionist consults her computer and offers them alternate times and treatments. The three make small talk, joke, laugh. They are becoming best friends. I glance at the clock again, gnashing my teeth.

Piano, piano is now out of the question: the time on the clock is 11:15. Finally, we reach the front of the line.

"*Bon giorno,*" Art says to the pretty receptionist.

"*Bon giorno,*" she answers.

"*No parlo Italiano,*" he says to her in perfect Italian. "*Parla inglese?*"

"Oh, sure," she says. "What can I help you with?" Her accent is New York.

"We *had* eleven o'clock appointments for a massage," he says.

"Name?" she asks.

Art gives her our names, she runs our credit card, and hands us two large, plastic bags, flip-flops, and locker keys. We head for the beaded doorway. On the other side, a mauve hallway displays two signs: "*uomo*" points to the right, "*donna,*" to the left. It seems we will part here.

"Remember," I say, "bathing suits for all treatments."

"*Piano, piano,*" Art trills. "Enjoy your massage." He ambles off.

I follow the arrow through another beaded opening and enter a room whose walls are lined with polished, high tech lockers. In the center of the room, four ottomans have been pushed together to form a sizable leather square that serves as a seating area. Despite the fact that this is only a changing room, it is a very elegant space.

There are two women in the room when I enter, both wearing the provided fluffy terry cloth robes. They're conversing in Italian, animated hands gesturing to aid communication. One's robe is tied at her waist. The other's is not and reveals a low cut, sequined bra and panties. I wonder if this is her bathing suit or her underwear. In either event, my nude-colored, modest Maiden Form undies are no couture match. On the spot, I decide not to expose my underwear to these chic Italian strangers. I find my locker, turn my back on them to disrobe, and tie the fluffy robe tightly around my waist.

The women disappear through a glass door that leads to a co-ed Jacuzzi where the soft chatter of Italian voices can be heard. I'm left alone, which makes me more comfortable, but presents me with a dilemma: I don't know where to go next. I'm feeling anything but *piano* when a dowdy, middle-aged woman steps through the beaded curtain.

I nod at her and she nods back. I suspect her underwear is no more glamorous than mine and feel at ease enough to ask for her help. By an exchange of gestures, she indicates I go upstairs to find my massage therapist. She points the way.

At the top of the stairs, Maria awaits. She is a short, chubby woman with streaks of gray running through her black hair. She has a sweet face. Using the same clear Italian Art used earlier, I tell her I don't speak her language. Her smile is forgiving. She puts her arm around my shoulders in a motherly fashion, and directs me toward a small room with a window that overlooks the park. She pats the massage table, indicating that I should lay down on it, face up, and she leaves the room. I climb onto the high table with some effort and conjecture that Italians who get massages must be tall.

Now relax, I tell myself. *Remember: piano.*

Sun pours through the slats of the shuttered window, warming the air in the room. I close my eyes and wait for Maria's touch. In the silence, I can hear her return and pull a chair up to the end of the massage table at my feet. She takes my left foot in her hand and makes a small, distressed sound. I open my eyes. She motions to my ankles, shows me that they are swollen. I know this. It happens when I travel. I nod at her, make some sympathetic noise, and settle back down. Maria spills oil into her hands and begins.

For the next twenty minutes, my left leg is in heaven. But the rest of my body is worried. Will it get attention, too? Will Maria have time for the right leg?

Maria stands to open the window. I hear the strings of the cello and drift off into the music. Finally, *piano*. I'm no longer concerned about the rest of my body getting its due or if Art wore a bathing suit facsimile. I'm not even worrying about what might happen when I hop down from this table with oil-slathered feet.

An hour after we've met, Maria and I hug good-bye like old friends. My ankles are back to their normal size, and I am completely relaxed.

"*Grazie, grazie mille,*" I say and meander back to the dressing room, passing fluffy-robed people wandering through purple-hazed walls. In a relaxed trance, I put on my street clothes.

I find Art waiting for me under an umbrella in the park.

"Shall we have lunch?" he asks.

In a restaurant with outdoor seating we order two glasses of Proseco. They arrive in frosted champagne flutes, very cold. Sipping the sparkling wine and waiting for our pasta to arrive, I ask Art, "How was your massage? What did you do about underwear?"

"I had a great massage from an attractive young *massaggia*," he says. I notice his Italian vocabulary has expanded. "And—I didn't wear underwear."

I raise my eyebrows.

"She gave me this," he says. With the slow movements of a strip tease artist, he extracts something blue from his shirt pocket. I stare at a paper thong.

"You wore *that?*"

"You know," he shrugs, *"piano, piano."* ❖

FICTION

Blue Waves

BY PATTY JOSLYN

I LOVE YOU LIKE CRAZY, this is what my mother said right before she drove herself, and me, into the Wachusett Reservoir. She, a woman who would not, could not, get her face wet in the shower. A woman soaked in fear, she wept through every swimming lesson she insisted I take. Each level a testament to her devotion.

Each achieved badge another sharp thing to scratch against my skin, to draw my own blood.

At reaching Level 4, which included a display of both the Butterfly and the Breaststroke, she took me out to dinner to celebrate. Halfway through her third glass of wine she got up to use the Ladies Room and never came back. It wasn't the first time, yet for me it felt like the last.

I fiddled with my new badge that resembled blue waves and a bowling pin, felt a warm spot of blood, and finally got up to call my dad.

My father grew up in Switzerland, a place of tall blonde relatives, with darling names attached to *their* swimming accomplishments. He tried to keep up with where I was—on any given day he would call me duck/swan/seal/frog (ente/schwan/seehund/frosch). He wondered, now, if he should use seahorse (seepferd) or ice bear (eisbar)?

I said, "Dad, I am a whale (wal)," and this is when I really started to bawl.

Now I know that advanced levels of one thing do not always align themselves with the heart.

Then, I was exhausted, standing, speaking softly into the phone, the smell of chlorine hanging from my damp hair and the beer rising from the soggy bar towel turned my stomach into somersaults. It was as it I was kicking off the pool wall to do yet another lap.

My dad lived in the city, my mom and I in the country, not too far from the reservoir I mentioned earlier. I knew my dad would tell me to sit tight, that he would be here as quick as he could. I knew the restaurant staff would try to make it seem as if this was the type of thing that happened all the time. I knew they would have me sit in a booth, out of the way, they would bring me limitless ginger ales. Did I want a cherry?

The whispers would be about me, about her. Thankfully they knew enough not to call the police. I suppose I looked older than I was. This, another thing attributed to my father and his genes. His heritage. Another thing my mother could not stand. Another thing that was driving her mad. Another reason to leave me again?

The other times I had waited and she had come back. Baby, Baby! she would say smelling like smoke and wine. Smelling like fog and damp earth. Tomorrow, she would say, we will make this right. Tonight, what we both need is sleep.

Those were the nights I would lie waiting for the morning light to show itself again.

Now, I have my own kids and I cannot forgive her.

Then, I would get up and make her coffee and toast, I would brush my teeth and hair, pack my lunch and my swimsuit, and kiss her goodbye.

How she spent her days I really do not know.

I only know that she loved me, like crazy, as she said herself, right before the car hit the water and I swam like a shark (hai), a dolphin (delfin) to set myself free. ❖

Non-Fiction

Queen of Cuts

by Kathleen Damiani

THIS STORY IS TRUE, at least most of it.
We were gathered one cold summer night at our friends' house in Fort Bragg to eat salmon fresh caught by the fishermen at Noyo Harbor; just the four of us, Tim and I, Cutler and DeeLynn. Unprepared for eating outdoors, I quickly became chilled in the evening fog. DeeLynn went inside and brought me a warm quilt. Admiring its beauty in the dimming light, I inspected the small pieces of fabric with their straight, ragged, circular, evenly cut or triangular edges. I ran my cold fingers over the textured prints of dramatic color, flowered or lined designs that filled in the 12 squares of the quilt, then wrapped it around me from my neck to below my knees.

I love quilts and have collected quite a few over the years from friends and family. I receive them as gifts and buy them for births, marriages, holidays and birthdays, from neighbors, quilters at Farmers' Markets and craft fairs, from the Amish, and from native women at the Pamunkey Indian Reservation near the Chesapeake Bay. Often, I hear from the quilt-maker the circumstances of its creation, her inspiration, the source and acquisition of the material, or the events occurring at the time.

It happened that the quilt warming my shivering body had a story to tell, too. This was no ordinary quilt (actually, none of them are ordinary). This was a millennial tribute quilt, a Y2K quilt. It was completed just before the transition to 2000. The idea, DeeLynn told me, began in Boston on the eastern end of our continent. As it journeyed west, the quilt plan spun a tale of itself, a story that wove in the characters who made it and the plot of its creation. The squares and pieces were cut, sewn and delivered across the United States: from Massachusetts to Missouri, Montana, Utah, and from southern and middle California, all the way north to Fort Bragg, where DeeLynn assembled and stitched this colorfully designed quilt.

A woman named Concessa, who lived in Boston, conceived the idea of a national Y2K quilt. DeeLynn first met her at an annual quilting retreat in Albion in 1996. Concessa hatched the idea and worked out the details over the next two years. The project took form as a sort of nod to Y2K, and to the millennial transition—a quirky, fun, yet highly organized wave of goodwill, a cheer and a toast to the 21st century. The quilts would express in texture, color, and fabric, a farewell to the past 1000 years. It was a way of joining hands and stitching the threads of women's lives across the country, as humanity prepared to leap across a man-made boundary. January 1st, 2000, is, after all, an arbitrary demarcation—a conceptual edge that cuts the cycles of the seasons into linear pieces—which humanity, through colonization and economics, bought into.

Since no one knew what lay on the other side of 1999, there was no plan for the finished quilts. The quilters could do what they wanted with theirs: hide under it, wave it around in the air, hang it on their door for protection, or just wrap themselves in it while the unknown crept up inevitably, with menace, a threat to the social order.

Concessa's plan was, simply put: 12 quilters, 12 fabrics, 12 blocks from each quilter, with Concessa organizing the project, which began in December of 1998, and finished in November of 1999. Twelve quilters from around the country participated, each sending Concessa three yards of a fabric of her choice. Concessa cut these 12 fabrics into "fat quarters" (22-inch x 18-inch), and made them into kits. She sent the kits of 12 varied "fat quarters" to each of the 12 quilters. During the months of the year preceding the millennium, each quilter would make one block for the other 11. The finished blocks were 12-inch square (a standard quilt block). Every quilter ended up with

12 blocks, composed of 12 different pieces of cloth from the other 11 women, plus her own. With these 12-inch finished squares, each of the 12 women stitched her own quilt.

In addition to the fabric, the quilters had to send out a brief bio about themselves. DeeLynn's began: "I'm writing this on the edge, here on the Pacific, where it never freezes and never gets hot …" DeeLynn was the only quilter from the northern California coast.

If you remember, the approach of the new millennium caught the attention of the world. We were collectively at the end of a 1,000-year cycle. The tech world shuddered with predictions of chaos and the collapse of communication, airline traffic control and transportation systems. From State Parks to State legislatures, to the media, universities, the offices of city managers and town supervisors, fire and police stations, military bases, airports and resorts, everyone muddled about in uncertainty. We guessed about the extent of damage, crisis and disaster this shift would cause in our sphere of responsibility, all due to a timing mechanism programmed into computers around the world. Special Y2K committees were hastily organized. Plans were made, memos sent out, preparations begun for the worst-case scenarios. New Agers, survivalists, and the conspiracy underground issued dire warnings and advice on acquiring first aid kits, storing water and provisions for families and pets. My psychic friends and the astrologers in my extended family were horrified to learn that my only preparation for my family was the purchase of an extra 5-lb bag of brown rice, just in case.

The day after our delicious evening barbecue with DeeLynn and Cutler, I was intrigued by the image of women stitching quilts in a project constellated around the number twelve. It was clear that the number was symbolic across many realms and dimensions of human life: 12 months of the year, 12 signs or constellations of the Zodiac, 12 astrological houses, 12 eras that earth crosses in a Platonic year (26,000 years), the 12 animals of the Chinese horoscope, etc. (This list is partial and does not include pages of biblical symbolism of the number 12).

Twelve, according to some, is also the number of completion, forming a whole, a perfect and harmonious unit, and, in some religions, expresses the Divine Mother.

What about 2012? Is it the year of completion, a telos, an edge of a new era? Or will it be a final termination—a collective backlash from the black goddess of all that was rejected in our era of wars: compassion and respect for life, the earth, cooperation to insure the safety and wellbeing of future generations?

My thoughts returned to the quilt. Since I never had the patience or skill to learn how to sew, embroider, or weave, I knew nothing about the subject of quilt-making. What I did know was the association of women with spinning and weaving and the archetypal feminine within the collective psyche.

I went to the Fort Bragg Library to do some research on the history of quilts. Overwhelmed by the scope of the subject and quilts' presence all over the world, their styles, and uses, I read only a portion of the material. (No pun intended.)

The definition of "quilting" is:

… the stitching together of layers of padding and fabric, may date back as far as ancient Egypt.

… In Europe, 12th c. Crusaders wore a quilted garment beneath their armour; remnants of the "Tristan" quilt made around 1360 still survive … Quilting was used in the fight to end slavery in the abolitionist movement; and as blankets for soldiers in the Civil War.

Up until the industrial revolution, most women had to spend a lot of time on spinning and weaving to provide fabric for their family's needs. Textiles were manufactured on a broad scale so commercial fabrics were affordable to almost every family by the 1840s. As a result, quilt making became widespread. (Wikipedia)

While all this was new to me, I was more curious about what preceded quilting: the spinning and weaving done by women around the world and its association in ancient times with the Fates—the spinning of the thread of life and its cutting. The boundaries of human life are, according to the archetypal record, in the hands of the goddesses. The primal, undomesticated goddesses of birth and death in the ancient near East remain active vibrationally as an archetype in the collective psyche, expressed in myths and fairy tales.

My goddess books were long gone, victims of black aspergillus mold. It was time to stock up again. I drove to the Gallery Bookshop in Mendocino and ordered a couple of excellent books on the goddess and symbols of the feminine I used to own and treasure: *The Woman's Dictionary of Symbols & Sacred Objects* by Barbara Walker and *The Myth of the Goddess: Evolution of an Image* by Anne Baring and Jules Cashford.

Describing the Great Mother, Baring & Cashford write that:

"(she) spins life out of herself, … As eternity spinning time, growth and destiny, she weaves the great web of life in the image of a mother with a child in her womb, who weaves life into form out of her body in ways still unknown to us. The Moirae, the three Greek goddesses of fate, born from the Underworld and Night…; the Cretan goddess of childbirth, Eileithyia; Athena; and Penelope waiting for Odysseus were all spinners and weavers of the threads of destiny, …" (p. 559)

After weeks of immersion in these books and other cherished books that survived the mold, especially *Themis* by Jane Ellen Harrison, synchronicity brought a kind of coherence between the act of cutting and edge-making and spinning the web of life. A goddess, not identified in any book, began to speak to me in dreams and waking reveries.

She called herself the "Queen of Cuts" and this is what she first told me:

I am she who cuts and snips
she who stops the sea with rock and cliff
she who crumbles the shore and swallows it

she whose fury smashes wind and water
thrashing off the edge of continents.

I oversee the cutting,
I remember what has been severed:
the amputated arm
the breast sliced off in mastectomy
the hundreds of millions of penis tips
sacrificed to the blind one, Yaldabaoth, the off-planet god.
I am the memory that cherishes what has been lost
re-weaving it into aliveness in the future.

I am the Dyad, Temple of Two,
the holy split whom philosophers loathe to discuss
For I cut and split the worlds
To make an I-Thou possible,
For sex to occur
For perception to arise
For Difference to radiate its light.

I am the space between you and nature
That allows you to see me stitch and re-stitch the Web of Life:
Cancelled, ignored and degraded by religion
Rejected by the off-planet god
Despised by the gurus and non-dual masters of illusion
Who dedicate their fear of mystery to an abstract one-ness—
The meme of "all-is-one"—whose purpose is to devour the simple-minded
And relieve them of the shock and demand of what stands naked and present before them.
I relate all things by separation and connection.
I never forget.

This announcement spoke herself in the darkness, at night, near the ocean of endings. I began to ponder all the prophecies of doom about the year 2012. We have arrived in 2012, and we were nearly at the winter solstice. In fact, it was almost 12-12-12. What could it mean? There were on-line sites devoted to the question. The Mayan calendar is supposed to end at the solstice, yet some researchers say that the hype is based solely on a smudgy collection of etchings on a rock in Guatemala. Some writers show evidence of the end of the "Platonic Year"—a cycle of 26,000 years. In Hinduism, we are at the end of the Kali-Yuga cycle, which does not bode well, for the Kali-Yuga is the darkest age of human depravity, the bottom of the pits in the cycle of world ages.

Our solar system is proceeding through a slow pole shift. Edgar Cayce and many of his students believed that our earth's changes would peak in 2012. Scientists claim that the cycle of mass coronal ejections from the sun will also peak, coinciding with the slow shift of the poles. This means earth will not be protected by its magnetic shield during a time of threat from solar ejections. Global warming is changing the surface of the earth with the melting of glaciers, the extremes of temperature, wild and unpredictable weather patterns, earthquakes, and volcanic eruptions, which no previous standards or charts are equipped to deal with.

Given that 2012 produced such a focus of attention, it became an edge—a possible ending. Yet, what is the year 2012, but an edge created by man, a concept? Why is our calendar unrelated to the natural world? Who decided time should start with an arbitrary zero—which cut our experience of history into two pieces, BC and AD (now called Common Era: before [BCE] or after (CE): i.e., before or after the zero. What purpose—whose agenda—was served to sever the bloodlines of our ancestral heritage from our Common Era? By whose authority was our ancient history—the "BC" time—castrated, cut off from the present, made into a "minus" number, non-existent except as an abstraction? Of what significance in nature, life or love is a "zero?"

We sailed successfully over the Y2K wave into the 21st century. What is 2012 but the inevitable arrival of an arbitrary edge created by religion? Perhaps one of the tragic results of this human edge-making is the loss and rejection of the continuity of the Mystery traditions that thrived in the "BC" years. There was a time when wisdom was spoken about on the streets, when sages instructed kings and princes how to rule wisely for the health, wellbeing and fecundity of their people, crops and animals.

We have endured the Age of Pisces over the last 2,000 years: an era of scapegoating, blood-letting, religious hatred and wars, of exploitation of the many for the gain of a few. Is it possible to cut a new edge in time? Can we invoke the Queen of Cuts, the Goddess of Two, to snip the threads that bind us to our bloody history? Can we stop humanity's march of repetition?

Maybe the hype and threats of doom about 2012 served a collective purpose. Perhaps we needed a new story for the next era, a new weaving of hearts and minds. Reading more about weaving, I came across two surprising notes in Wikipedia that address the question of humanity's fate in 2012:

"The concept of weaving actually relates to mythology much more than simply appearing in myths. The English word text is derived from the Latin word for weaving, texare, explaining the source of terms like 'weaving a story.'"

Or will our alternate fate be in the hands of the Valkyries:

"…women weaving on a loom, with 'severed heads for weights, arrows for shuttles, and human gut for the warp, singing an exultant song of carnage.'" ❖

"Bishop Pine," Janet Ashford

Flying Instructions

by Cheri Ause

Disambiguation could be
another word for *tightrope walking:*
"to remove any ambiguity"—a useful idea
when you're poised on one square foot of heaven
tucked up in the tip of the big top
and working without a net.

Upturned faces swirl below,
teeth chattering like tumbling dice,
eyes glittering like flashing knives,
mouths splitting into a gaping red O.

This is what they've come for
to behold the beauty of grace and form
to admire the art of the subtle move
and maybe, just maybe,
to taste one sip from the cup of disaster,
or tongue some small morsel of tragedy.

Because falling is the easy part
and when that happens   and it will
only skill can save.

Like the Flying Wallendas.

One summer night in Akron they tumbled
to their most magnificent failure.
The morning paper said they fell so gracefully
it was as if they were flying.

But that was years before Detroit
Before the seven-chair pyramid collapsed
—two dead, one paralyzed—
before Rietta and Chico then Karl,
before the causalities began piling up
like crushed kewpie dolls behind the midway.

Because if you lose your nerve, nothing can save.

So you hone your craft until the time comes
when you stand alone above the crowd,
bruised, perhaps, but not broken,
no harlequin illusion of safety swaying beneath you,
your fate balancing on a golden wire
stretched between you and that bright spot
just beyond the chasm.

In that moment there's nothing left to do
but raise your arms, press your toes
to the tip of your rosin-soft slippers,
grip the razor's quivering edge,
and put one foot in front of the other.

Fiction

Suspended Animation

by Jan Edwards

A ONCE-FAMOUS ACTRESS in the twilight of her career was forced by her finances to accept a minor role, playing a crazy aunt in a Broadway play. After years of star billing she felt devalued, and made a bet with the crew that she could steal a scene from the young leading lady without even being on the stage. So, before curtain time, she sneaked onto the set where stood a small table holding glasses and a water pitcher. She put double-stick tape on the bottom of one glass.

In the second act this aging actress made her entrance and delivered her part with a trademark flourish. Before her exit, she picked up the glass and slowly filled it with water. She set it down with its bottom hanging half-off the table edge. The glass looked unstable, as if it could fall at any moment, while actually it was secure thanks to the hidden tape.

When the young actress entered to play her big scene, she was destined to flop. No matter how grandly she gestured or deeply she emoted, the audience would not respond because no one was watching her. Every eye was fixed on that glass of water.

The story usually ends here with the young actress foiled by an old magic trick, the audience shown to be gullible sheep, and the bet won by the old master performer. But there is much more to tell, particularly about the young actress who was the target of the stunt, the one the critics called "the fresh new face of 1935." Her name was Margot Montague.

As Margot stepped onto the stage that evening, she sensed the atmosphere was charged, but assumed it was the effect of her charisma.

She began her soliloquy and was through the first half of the speech before realizing the audience was not with her. The enhanced energy, which should rightfully be hers, was directed upstage. Stopping mid-word, she turned. When she saw the water glass hanging in suspense, she became transfixed.

After a moment, she regained her wits and walked softly toward the table. As she tiptoed closer to the glass she noticed the tape. It wasn't hard to guess who did it and why. But before she could get angry, Margot had an artistic revelation. On one level this was a silly prank by a jealous has-been; on another, it was the essence of theater.

Since she was near the glass, the audience followed her every move. Margot dipped her finger in the water and ran it around the rim. The glass sang out its high-pitched note. The audience gasped: they were hers.

This was a play, however, and it must go on. Margot was careful to hide the tape from view as she lifted the glass, then moved it back to the safe center of the table. The audience applauded and she took a mock bow before strolling downstage to finish the scene.

Back in her dressing room, Margot combed out her platinum waves while mulling over the lesson of the glass. These people paid to see a play, so why did they prefer to watch a trick? Because they did not know it was a trick. They thought it was true. But many things are true and few could capture an audience like this; they were spellbound.

Margot tuned her mind back to the moment when she first saw the glass hanging off the edge. What had so fascinated her? The surprise first: then wondering why the glass didn't fall, and when it would fall, and what would happen when it finally fell? Had she hoped it would fall? Yes, she had to admit she had. She was not able to take her eyes off that glass for fear she would miss seeing it happen.

If something so simple could mesmerize the masses, perhaps she could learn to use it to enhance her own stage presence—but how? She thought of nothing else all the next day. To design such a focusing technique would take trial and error. Ideally, to captivate the audience there should be an extended period of suspense, and it must directly involve her person.

The next evening, Margot made her second act entrance in a gown with a few alterations. The thin straps on the left shoulder had been cut almost through. When she made a sweep of her arm they snapped and the bodice dropped the intended amount, since it was stitched invisibly to the undergarment. The gimmick worked; the audience gasped as they had the night before. All eyes stayed riveted to the broken straps for the rest of the scene.

It was an easy win, she knew. No different from a vaudeville act or a striptease, and not quite the sort of focus she was after. Nothing she could risk repeating; this was legitimate theater, after all. But the promise of absolute attention from hundreds of eyes was tempting. To perfect her theory, over the next few weeks she conducted risky experiments. She spoke her lines with eyes closed, while pacing the apron edge, threatening with every step to fall into the pit. An electrician agreed to drop a Fresnel during her scene, leaving it dangling dangerously over her head. She hired the carpenter to rig a chair with one leg missing, teasing the audience that she was about to sit on it, until finally she did.

The crowd was delighted, but the director was not. He was paying for dramatic performances, not high-wire circus acts. He demanded she quit the stunts or he would find another actress who respected theater as art. In a fit of temper, Margot walked out on the show.

At that moment, though she didn't know it, Margot Montague stood on the cutting edge. She had stumbled onto what would become the entertainment revolution of the century, and women from the Gabors to the Kardashians would follow her lead.

The water glass experiments had given her insights. No longer would she be merely a movable prop mouthing the words of others. Margot intended to write her own story with her life as her stage. Her passion had been distilled. She needed to be watched, nothing more. And she now knew what fascinated people. Not carefully crafted speeches recited on stage in rounded tones, but true life: true danger, true drama, true romance, or at least what those watching believed to be true.

Her agent was eager to orchestrate the spin. *Mysterious illness causes rising star to drop out of hit show,* read the release. The photo spread of Margot looking pale but lovely in peach silk lounging pajamas created a fashion trend. Newsreels reported on her baffling symptoms and the get well cards poured in. Doctors offered tonics, treatments, and therapies. Margot, basking in attention, plotted her recovery.

First, she must approach death's door. The press release announced that, after taking a drastic turn, Miss Montague had been admitted to the Golden Phoenix Sanitarium. There, under the care of the brilliant young Dr. Osbourn, she underwent a dangerous new procedure, never before tried. It was her last hope and the young doctor never left her side, except to give hourly reports on her condition to a worried world.

Once it was announced that Margot would live, the recovery was rapid and complete. Her spring back to radiant health (and into the arms of the doctor who saved her) was one for the annals of medicine. Reporters declared it a miracle.

Romance was rumored when the dashing Dr. Osbourn and Margot Montague were spotted cheek to cheek at the Stork Club. A photo of the happy couple made the cover of *Screen Stars,* although Margot had never made a movie.

Her agent urged a relapse, but Margot decided the fans craved a wedding. A date was quickly set. Magazines ran shots of her in designer gowns so readers could vote on their favorite. Honeymoon options were weighed in the press as though national interests were at stake. The guest list was leaked and read like *Who's Who in New York*.

Meanwhile, Margot planned her last minute exit from the engagement. The good doctor turned out to be a cold fish. He was hard to convince to go dancing, worried constantly about his sanitarium, and couldn't wait to get back to Arizona, of all places. Should she dump him now or leave him at the altar?

The agent was horrified. She had to go through with the wedding or the press would tear her to shreds. The man had saved her life, for God's sake, plenty of time to get out of it later. This time Margot heeded his advice. She glided down the aisle at Saint Patrick's glowing like an angel. People waited on the sidewalk with their bags full of rice, soaking through their hankies.

Newsreels followed the honeymoon through Paris, Venice and Rome. They arrived home on the *Queen Mary* to a smattering of well-wishers at the dock. The newlyweds settled into a ranch style home outside Phoenix, but after a few women's magazines examined the furnishings and asked for Margot's favorite recipes, the spotlight faded. With no trendy night spots, no opera galas to attend, what was she supposed to do, take up horseback riding, join the country club?

The idea to have a baby belonged to her agent. There's dramatic potential no matter how things turn out, he told her. Planning to be tragically barren, Margot agreed to hint that she and the doctor were "trying." As luck would have it, she got pregnant within the month. The surrounding publicity was mild since in those days women hid their baby bumps. The birth was normal, unfortunately, and after a few cute shots of her with the baby, she found the press disinterested.

Motherhood didn't suit her. Everyone focused on the baby instead of her. Even her husband was smitten with the brat. Margot wanted nothing more than to get out of that ranch house and back to New York. This time the agent would not dissuade her. As soon as she got her figure back, she began to set up her escape.

Though the good doctor didn't know it, he was about to be caught in an affair. The pictures showed, without a doubt, him entering a hotel with that woman. No amount of pleading innocence could save him, not while the tears of his heartbroken wife snatched the headlines.

After a quick trip to Reno, Margot bought a penthouse on Central

Park with the proceeds from the sale of the sanatorium. She was generous to leave the ranch house for the doctor, who needed some place to raise the kid.

Back at last, she hit the clubs, making sure to be at the right table when the bulbs flashed. A gay divorcee with a different beau every night, designers begged her to wear their hats. Restaurants never charged her, hoping for the publicity that trailed in her wake. Jewels, furs and cars were free for the asking because, if Margot Montague didn't have it, it wasn't worth having. That went for friends as well. A party wasn't a party without Margot on the list.

Over the years she turned down numerous offers to go back to the stage, but when Hollywood called she jumped on a train to California. She had always thought her life would make a marvelous movie and she planned to play herself. But when she arrived, the offer mysteriously dissolved. It's 1942, and we're in a war, she was told; tastes have changed. No one mentioned it, but she had also changed. Late night parties had taken their toll on her famous creamy complexion. Admirers found her still attractive at 33, but film is not so charitable.

Since she arrived in Hollywood with great fanfare, she decided to stay for the season. She spent weekends at Hearst Castle, sunned herself on the beach at the Hotel Del Coronado, and went to the races with Jimmy Durante. But it was at supper one night at the Zanuck's house that she met Frank Reilly, the man who would be her downfall.

Frank, an up-and-coming actor, had just been drafted and was heading overseas. The dinner party was in his honor, and they had him seated next to their other special guest, Margot Montague. The two hit it off and, as was common with soldiers heading into hell-storms, he proposed after only a few dates. Margot must have been off her game, because she got swept up in the romance. They were married by a justice of the peace and drove all night to an inn overlooking the sea on the rugged north coast. Four bittersweet days later he shipped out.

The press got onto it late, since Margot had forgotten to call her agent. There were only a few snapshots of the couple, but the country was starved for feel-good stories involving servicemen. Frank was a handsome guy and Margot still had sizzle. Soon she was back in the magazines, this time as the war wife waiting for her man. It's the perfect angle for wartime, her agent told her. But for Margot it was no angle, it was true.

She helped sell war bonds, served cookies to GIs at the Hollywood Canteen, and wrote letters to Frank twice a day. She was planning a USO tour when the telegram arrived. Her knees weakened when she saw the envelope; she sank down on the chaise to read the brief, impersonal text. She stayed there frozen for over an hour, holding the yellow paper in her hand.

For a week she wandered around the house, stopping a dozen times a day to reread the words, hoping they had changed. Then one day she picked up the telegram, tied the silk scarf Frank had sent from London around her hair, and pulled the Continental out of the garage. The top was down and the wind caused her eyes to tear, as she raced up the state. The sky was turning orange by the time she reached their inn. She checked into their cabin.

The cliff in front of the cabin had a sheer drop to the rocks and waves below. Margot blindfolded her eyes with the scarf and began to walk the edge. She was able to take eight steps on solid ground before she lost her footing.

News of the suicide of Margot Montague would not be comforting to a nation of war wives and was hushed up. What could have been a huge media event and her crowning achievement passed with hardly a notice.

Margot didn't leave a note, just the telegram, which read: Lieutenant Frank Reilly was reported missing in action. Below that in a shaky hand was written: We are each of us a glass teetering on the edge. Only her agent knew what it meant. ❖

Non-Fiction

24 Hours

BY LEW MERMELSTEIN

So far, April 23, 1973, looked like a normal Monday afternoon at Addis Ababa's Bolé International Airport. All the passengers and taxis were gone. There were no more flights today. Three guards in drab olive green uniforms squatted in the shade of eucalyptus and pine trees and chatted about yesterday's football game. The rainy season started last week, washing away six months of dry season's stagnant dusty haze. The sweet scent of eucalyptus and pine filled the air. Vultures cawed and soared on afternoon thermals, re-claiming their space. Above them, billowing white clouds heaved and tossed in a shimmering blue sky.

A blue and white World Health Organization Toyota Land Cruiser entered the loop in front of the terminal. It slowed, but didn't stop. The right headlight dangled from its socket, jumping with each lurch and swerve as the driver and passenger struggled for control of the steering wheel. When it finally did stop, the passenger grabbed his bags and hit the ground running.

"Steve! Wait, Steve!" Duke yelled.

But it was too late. Steve was gone, heading right for the security fence. Duke Peters, stout, muscular, Small Pox Eradication Peace Corps Volunteer, was supposed to keep an eye on Steve until Max got back. If he needed help, he could call the Peace Corps office. Men make plans—God laughs.

Steve Williams, Agricultural Extension Agent from western Ethiopia and recently resigned Peace Corps Volunteer, threw his sleeping bag over the chain link fence and onto the field of idle airplanes. One of the guards, who had been arguing with another about a blocked kick at Sunday's football game, jumped to his feet and pointed at the wild-eyed, bearded white guy climbing over the fence. Steve grabbed his sleeping bag and ran towards the US Embassy's Military Airlift Command C-141 "escape plane." One guard tackled him meters from his goal. Another pushed his rifle into Steve's back, forcing him to the tarmac.

"Wend'em-may, Wend'em-may." Brothers, brothers, he called out in perfect Amharic. When Amharic didn't work, Steve, thinking they were from the west, tried speaking to them in Gallinya.

"Mah no?" Who are you? They demanded in Amharic.

"Your friend," Steve answered. "My name is Girma." This was the Amharic name given to Steve in language training. Steve's middle name was Jeremiah—close to Girma, which means wonderful. "I'm going to Washington tomorrow. I'm going to tell Congress all about the corruption in Ethiopia. I just wanted to sleep on the plane tonight. Honest." Steve pleaded in that high whiny voice, the same voice he used when he tried to get you to do something you really didn't want to do. Steve was always at the edge, but this time he'd gone too far.

Vultures cawed and watched from above. The chain-link fence rattled as Duke shook it in disbelief, watching them pull Steve up and march him away. He hid against the wall and held back any sound his mouth wanted to make. Sweat and tears ran down his face to his Fu Manchu mustache where his tongue tasted fear. He only had minutes until more guards showed up. He ran to the pay phone in the lobby of the terminal and called the Peace Corps office.

A camouflaged Land Rover, followed by a truck filled with some of the toughest soldiers on the planet, roared into the airport loop, sirens blaring. From the Land Rover, officers barked commands into walkie-talkies. "See if there are any other *ferenjis.*"

As Duke waited for the call to go through, he saw Steve being marched to the Land Rover. "Damn." When he finally got through to the Peace Corps office it was MR who answered and not Maria.

Oh no! No time for her bullshit. Gotta' get through her. Gotta' talk to Wally right now.

"MR? Hi. It's Duke Peters. I've got to speak to Wally Lisbon."

"Sure you do," she sang out. "Everybody wants to talk to Wally. He's busy," she barked.

"Tell him it's an emergency. Tell him it's about Steve. He's been arrested at Bolé airport."

Duke felt a sharp jab in his back. The guards had no trouble finding him. He was the only other *ferenji* in the airport. One guard pointed his rifle at Duke's face, another grabbed the phone and hung up.

MR knocked on Wally's door.

"This better be important." Wally spoke in a rising pitch.

Wally Lisbon was a tall, handsome forty-something, who usually looked as if he just stepped off a tennis court. Back in upstate New York, the Lisbon family was a major contributor to the President's campaign. Wally got to spend the next few years in Addis Ababa at a damn good Civil Servant salary, with lots of perks, including maid service at their residence. Wally was usually the Program Officer, but since the Chief was back in DC that made him Acting Director. Right now he was composing a letter to Steve Williams' older brother, asking him to meet his *distraught* (Wally struggled for the perfect adjective) brother in DC in a few days. The details were sketchy. Max Aaronson and Duke Peters were to accompany Steve back to DC under the pretense that they were going to Congress to, as Steve kept saying, "spill the beans" about all the corruption in Ethiopia.

"Wally, I hate to bother you, but I got a strange call from Duke Peters. He said Steve Williams was just arrested at Bolé Airport."

Wally's pen froze.

"Oh shit! What else did he say?"

"That's all he said and then the phone went dead."

Wally stood at his desk, mumbling to himself. "I can't believe this is happening. That crazy bastard!" He called out. "What the hell did he do now?"

"Should I try to call Max?" MR asked.

"Yeah. Call the embassy. He might still be there."

MR went back to her office.

"What the hell is going on?" Wally said softly.

He sat at his desk, a white tennis sweater draped across his shoulders, and stared straight ahead at the office door, the same door that burst open last Wednesday when Steve Williams charged into his office and smacked down a manila envelope.

"I resign, Wally. You can take this fucking Peace Corps bullshit and shove it. I'm outa' here." The slamming door rattled the building as Steve stomped out. Wally caught up with him as he waited for one of those little blue and white Fiat taxis in front of the Peace Corps office.

"Steve! Steve!"

Steve didn't answer, and kept trying to wave down a taxi.

"Let's talk, Steve."

"I got nothing to say. It's all in my letter."

Wally had the envelope with him and opened it. There were several pages written in Amharic. The only thing Wally could make out was on the last page. It was signed, "ex-PCV Steven Jeremiah Williams." The "ex" was underlined several times, each slash more angled.

"Steve, I can't read this," Wally said. "It's all in Amharic. What's it say?"

"Give it to Maria. She'll translate it for you."

Maria, the Chief's secretary, was a stunning example of Amharic motherhood and Italian fatherhood, as beautiful as she was cheerful. Soft, straight black hair framed her auburn face, delicate lips and captivating angelic eyes; it flowed river-like across her shoulders, down her white fleece sweater, and sprayed off her two supple breasts. It was all Wally could do to restrain himself.

"Wally?" said MR.

Wally was lost in thoughts of marital infidelity and multi-cultural fantasies.

"Wally? Wally!" MR called out.

The room came back into focus. "What is it?" he said as he cleared his throat and straightened himself.

"Better pick up the phone, Wally. It's the Ambassador."

"Yes, Mister Ambassador. Ministry of Interior. Right now, sir. Of course."

Max Aaronson, Rural Electrification Engineer PCV, had just left the US Embassy after getting passports, travel authorizations and some US cash, in preparation for their big flight back to DC tomorrow with Steve and Duke. Engineer that he was, Max had the whole thing under control. They would escort Steve back to Peace Corps DC, take a week at home, Max to Pittsburgh, Duke to New Haven, and then back to Addis. Things were going as he planned.

What Max didn't know was that while he was driving to check-in with Steve and Duke, Steve and Duke were in the camouflaged Land Rover with flashing red lights that passed him, going the opposite direction, heading to the Ministry of Interior for interrogation.

When Wally got to the Ministry of Interior, the Ambassador came out the front door, speaking through a translator with the Vice-Minister of Internal Security, a nephew of Haile Selassie. The Ambassador gestured that he understood, thanked him and headed off to see Wally.

"They've got two of your volunteers in there. They say one of them is crazy like a wild man. The other one's shaking like a leaf. So far, no one's been accused of anything, but they're talking about charging the crazy one with attempted hijacking. Wally," the Ambassador got into Wally's face and exhaled hotly. "What the hell is going on?"

Wally was about to explain, but said, "Later. Here comes the translator."

The translator bowed courteously. "After careful consideration, His Imperial Majesty's Government has graciously agreed to drop all charges if you get the crazy one out of Ethiopia within twenty-four hours." ❖

Non-Fiction

Mother's Ire

BY MARYLYN SCOTT

WHEN I HEARD Mother had been moved to a nursing home, nothing mattered but being with her. I purchased a plane ticket to Philadelphia, and a rental car. I was against moving Mother out of her Pocono Mountains home. My sister Dottie was named executor; she was in charge. To be fair, Dottie could not take care of Mother from a hundred miles away. I was even further—on the opposite side of the country. Be that as it may, Dottie did not invite discourse on the subject.

I went directly to the nursing home. There she was, my mother, lying on her back, oxygen tube in her nose, her eyes closed. Another woman lay in the bed next to hers. Partially curtained separation. An unwatched television droned.

My sister whispered. "She won't know you."

I leaned toward Mother's face. Traces of beauty, still apparent, woven into a lifetime of lines. Smiles. Frowns. I smiled, speaking softly. "Hello, Mother."

Her blue-gray eyes opened, looked directly into mine. "Why, hello Marylyn," she said.

Mother always prefaced her hello with "why." Surprise and delight. I took her hand. She took mine. That was the lifeline. Neither of us let go.

Dottie kept saying I should leave her alone. "She needs her rest."

I couldn't think why. Rest waited rather completely on the Other Side. But I said nothing. Mother held on more tightly. We continued to hold each other's hand all week.

The staff came in regularly, to give her "medicine." They worked it into her mouth despite the laboring of her tongue to push away the spoon.

"Mnp. Mnp," she mumbled, trying to close her mouth. And soon, nodded off.

"There," the attendant would say. "Now she can sleep."

"What is it?" I asked.

"Something to help her rest." The attendant looked at me blankly.

"Narcotic?" I asked.

"Yes. It is."

When Mother awoke, I asked her if she liked the medicine. Her eyes displayed a flash of that old anger. Frightening in my younger days. Now, a comforting spark.

"No," she said. " … don't want it." With someone here to listen, she went on. "… want to go home."

Mother was always meticulous with language, making it say exactly what she wanted. Emotions underlined her words. "Speak clearly," she would admonish me. "Dot your i's. Cross your t's." It was odd to hear her leave out her own "I." Now "I" was barely there.

When the attendant came into the room, I told her. "Mother doesn't want the narcotic. She wants to stay awake."

"Doctor's orders," the attendant said brightly. I felt that familiar flash spark in me. Subduing it, I asked to speak to the doctor and was, mutely, led into the corridor to a desk.

The prescribing doctor offered weak rationale. It was routine.

"My mother does not want to take narcotics. She didn't opt for it in her life; she doesn't want it now. She wants to be with me. I want to be with her."

He smiled at me and said OK.

The attendants continued to try, routinely, to give her the narcotic.

"No," I said. "Doctor's orders."

Toby and Trynt, my two eldest children—Mother's first two grandchildren—came to be with her. They took turns holding her hand while I ate or slept a bit. Mother's happiness at having all three of us there could be felt in the silence, punctuated by nods or no's to our occasional questions regarding her need or comfort. Water? Want to eat a little?

Punctuated by her quiet declarations. "I want to go home."

The attendants patted her on the head or arm, shoved the medicine in her mouth when they could, and told her. "Yes. You're going home."

"When?"

"Soon." They didn't mean the same home my Mother meant. Underneath my calm exterior, a lifetime of disagreement with The System in general, the posturing of professionals and the somewhat professional, the therapeutic "lie," even my sister's assumption of correctness, threatened to burst out of the containment in which it was held.

"Now." Mother said. "I want to go home now."

Even with a bit of resignation in the tone, you could tell, Mother meant it.

Given the opportunity, I would have gone to Stroudsburg and let her pass at home where the spirit and memory of loved ones were contained in photos and relics, and visits from loyal and still-living friends. As it was, her friends had to absorb the loss of her without saying goodbye, without a chance to speak everyday words, or later, to speak in presence and in memory. Dorothy, my mother, simply disappeared from their lives.

I haven't seen Dorothy for a while. Have you? No. I hear she went to live with her daughter. I hear she went to a nursing home. I hear she died. I liked her. She was always so cheerful. She was sweet. She always remembered my birthday. I miss her. She always came on Fridays to have her hair done.

Back and forth to the nursing home we went. Within a few days, the other bed was empty. A comfort to be alone and together in the room. A discomfiting projection of things to come. I slept in the extra bed rather than go back to Dottie's. I did not want to miss the moment of passing.

I'd been with dying people before. Maggie. I saw the soul rise from the top of her skull, a grayish purple plume, spiraling up. For a brief moment, it was still, as if trying to figure out the lay of the new landscape, then continued its ascent. I stayed for a good hour, until I felt certain the plume—her soul as I chose to identify it, had ascended.

With Jack, I saw sulphur roil furiously above his head. The VA attendants had narcotized him to near-death. I caught him as he keeled over on our way to the cafeteria. Put him in the wheel chair. Sat the Watch, crooning and holding hands. I saved him that time from Death.

He rallied and I inquired. "Are you ready to go?"

"No. Not yet."

"Okay, then. You have to refuse the narcotics." And he did. The staff, figuratively, raised their fingers in the sign of a cross. I had created a spell. He had risen from the dead. Not only that, I questioned procedure, not for the first time. I took it to the Director. I was blowing a whistle, making them nervous.

Restored to the point of relative ease, Jack opted to leave the hospital for a few hours. We went to the Balboa Street Cafe for mochas and a pastry. We drove to the ocean, stared at the waves, smoked a joint, not really caring to dwell on whether or not this was the last anything. We stayed in the presence of undying love and laughed.

I talked to him about his druthers. Why here at the V. A. Hospital? He said they were repaying him for his military service. I suggested he go home. "Have things the way you want them." He did. He went home. Friends and family came and went and came and stayed. Hospice offered what prescription drugs he might need and sometimes want. Mostly he wanted pot, talk, music. He passed in the middle of the night, friends and family all around.

With mother, I kept looking for an indication, for that bit of soul that would let me know something. It never came. My kids needed to go back home. Mother did not want to say goodbye and mourned their absence. I drove them to the airport. On the way, we took in the Philadelphia Museum of Art, at a run, and ate a quick but lovely meal. A memory tour of younger days.

I returned to the nursing home. Nothing had changed. It was late at night. The bed next to Mother's filled again. I needed to sleep. The attendant came in to give medicine.

"She doesn't want it," I said.

"Just a little," she said. "To help her sleep," and shoved the narcotic into her mouth.

"Mnnp. Mnnp." Mother was dozing when I kissed her goodbye, though I felt the tightening of her grip telling me to stay.

The need for sleep won. I looked into the attendant's eyes. I felt Mother's flash ignite my words and spoke clearly. "Call me right away if anything *whatsoever* changes. I'll come right over."

It was near 5:00 a.m. when the phone rang. I jumped to answer it. A voice spoke, telling me Mother had passed. Disappointment and anger waged a war within me. "I'll be right there." Dottie came, too.

I held Mother's hand. I wanted to see. I wanted to feel. Something of soul, of spirit, something that lingered. But there was nothing. She was gone. Glad to be free. Flying home to Stroudsburg. I could see her, flying low over the rushing water, putting her hands into the soil where the bulbs she planted slept in the dark of winter, calling to her cat, touching the precious artifacts of her life. Into the stormy sky she rose to meet those elements that played in her blue-gray eyes, that flash of indignant ire.

I had seen other colors in her eyes. Blue-green like summer sky and growing things. Twinkling sunlight. Moody moonlight. But these were not what she would now show. She would not meet Death with sunlight and smiles. No, it would be flashes of lightning, dark and ominous clouds, indignant challenge. Conscious choice of meeting what is unknown. ❖

"Point Cabrillo," Janet Ashford

Fiction

Outlaw Ford

by Malcolm Macdonald

Chapter One: California

I'VE BEEN CHEATING THE FATES right from the start.

The night I was born, Ma, Pa, and big sister Cal played cutthroat pinochle by lantern light in the log house of my youth. Ma held a winning hand when the labor pains hit, wouldn't lay down her cards 'til she made her bid.

A storm rumbled the sky while they helped Mother to the tracks and onto the handcar. Pa and Cal pumped the handles down the rail line toward the Company House.

According to Ma, "You shot right out in the rain, bounced clean over the edge. Pulled you back, yanking hand over fist on your cord."

"Lucky to be alive," they said at the Company House when Pa carried us in. Not one, or two, but three midwives there, the Fair sisters: Lacey, Chloe, and Atropos. They managed the lumber company's guesthouse and restaurant. Cal waited tables there.

Thunder clapped and Pa said, "God's applauding the birth of my son."

Chloe Fair spun her thread. "It's God alright, shooting craps across the high heavens."

Her sister Lacey measured me head to toe. "Beelzebub's betting the Almighty can't save this baby's soul."

"Who'll win?" Cal asked.

Atropos, who'd snipped my cord, looked up from beside the couch where they'd laid Ma and little me. "Too soon to tell."

Lightning struck all around; New Year's Eve, New Year's morn.

Nineteen hundred, nineteen-ought-one, flip a coin; take your pick. With all the fanfare you'd think I'd get more attention, but Ma was back at the stove next day. I got a makeshift bassinet in a corner of the kitchen.

Sister Cal wasn't born there, but back on the farm in Kansas. The folks lived their ambitions and humor in their children's names: California, Nevada (born in Nebraska), Louis (for Louisiana), Ida (for Idaho), and off they went. In California, Moreland, Orland and I were born. Cal called me Les right off, never Lester. Mother and Father, they had their mirth. Three boys in a row: More, Or, Les.

After we all rolled out, I wasn't more or less, but right in the middle, so's you'd hardly notice: six older, six younger.

Father's brother, Nolan, taught me how to play cards. Scarcely could walk and talk when he showed me how to shuffle a deck and other tricks of the trade. Soon I was playing rummy with Chloe and Lacey Fair whenever Ma went to town.

Next time Nolan showed at home, I boasted. "Double dealt. They never knowed. And I bested 'em."

Ma overheard, slapped my hands and said, "That's cheating. No. No!"

She scowled at Uncle, but when her back was turned he whispered. "Anything goes when you have to play Fair."

Father chopped in the woods six days a week. Sundays, camp meeting. Preacher came, riding the circuit, read the words, led the hymns, gave the look for all to say amen.

One Sunday afternoon when I was four, Father walked me down the railroad track. His hand held mine while we strode toward Dead Man's Curve: big bend in the river, sharp turn of the rails.

On a slope above the bend, a picket fence surrounded Dead Man's Cemetery; three unnamed markers. "Shot in that cabin." Father pointed up the hill. "Playing at cards, wild wagers on a moonless night."

I looked up to my father, who said, "Never gamble on cards, boy … When you do, don't wager more than you can afford to lose. Always play to win, but let the other fellas slink away with a little something jingling in their pockets."

We walked around the fence once or twice, patting every picket. "Death's never a stranger 'round here, boy. Seldom sends ahead to let you know he's coming."

A few days later, I played with an old deck underneath the dining room table of the Company Guest House while Cal cleared the plates; all three Fairs too busy for me. Dealt out cards to an imaginary opponent, changing the rules to my own brand of War so I always won.

The front door banged open against the wall. Dishes smashed to the floor all around and Cal wailed. A young steamship captain staggered in carrying a man in his arms, their shirts smeared with drying blood and more seeping from an unseen wound. Both men disappeared while the captain set the injured man on the tabletop. All I saw were polished boots. "Log flew off at Deadman's, Miss," the captain said to Cal. "Hit him flush."

Blood flooded the tablecloth and dripped from the fringed edges onto my jokers and aces. The injured man slammed a hand down and called, "Jesus! Help me."

He didn't come, unless the Company House cook was Jesus Christ. In which case you'd think he'd make a better vegetable beef soup.

Blood swamped my entire deck. The injured man let out a prolonged groan. The table shook, wobbled to a standstill, followed by a longer quiet.

The captain and Cal clasped hands together, spoke some holy words and amens. The cook said, "Death's got him now."

Felt a shiver run right through me. The front door slammed shut. I scrambled from under the table, but by the time I swung the big redwood door open, Death was out of sight.

I started going to Dead Man's Cemetery almost every day after my chores were through. Pitched pennies against the rails, leaned over the fence looking for new headstones.

One afternoon I caught a splinter in my palm. Big brother Louis ambled along while I tried to pinch it out. "Whatcha doin' down here?" he asked.

"Guardin' the gate, so Mr. Death doesn't put Pa in with the dead men."

"There's no Mr. Death."

"You sure?"

"No, but if there is, he'd be a lot sneakier than you give him credit for; wouldn't be hiding out at the graveyard. That's not where people die, it's where they go after they're dead."

I popped the sliver out along with a trickle of blood then spit in my palm. Louis daubed it dry with a corner of his shirttail. I asked, "If he don't come here, why doesn't everybody live in a graveyard?"

The river, that river, first river of my childhood; crammed with logs near the harbor. The grey-green water at Deadman's Curve banked by hills cut clear and brown: made the river look wider. Cal, the only one of us taught to swim. The Dillard boy got caught under the logs. Mother said, "If you go an' get yourself drowned dead, don't come crying home to me."

Long straight stretch to the next bend upstream from Deadman's; fields of grass growing wide on either side, reeds blending into clover. Company cattle grazed beneath a trestle that ran away from the water into a dark gulch of redwood yet to be felled.

Company beef: for the camp cook's pot, for the hungry plates at the Guest House; folks up from 'Frisco chewing tender, gnashing tough; captains of freighters waiting to be laden with their precious timber cargo.

Learned both those words, cargo and laden, from Captain Freeman. He came from Norway with a name too hard to pronounce and told the immigration man, "I'm a free man in America."

I got to eat lunch beside him at the Guest House, if I didn't bother Cal while she served. The Captain always lifted his spoon ever so carefully over his bowl of soup. Never saw him spill.

Lost his accent right away in the States, but when he laughed I heard the Norseman sunk low in his throat. "Do you know the name of my vessel?"

He answered himself. "The Shroud of Fog."

He laughed and I looked beyond his thick, gleaming teeth for a horn-headed Viking I'd seen in a picture book. Cal filled his water glass. The Captain studied her smile. "If I hit the rocks and go to Davy Jones' Deep, I want it said I went down in a shroud of fog." His ocean eyes followed Cal. He nudged me and grinned. "Nice excuse for my epitaph."

Cal glanced away, so I pushed my cracker crumbs onto the floor. "Captain, what's an epitaph?"

"It's a saying writ on your grave, Les, a saying that sums up all your life and deeds." He leaned forward and lowered his voice. "Sometimes, you have to lie a little to get at the truth."

Cal was my favorite sister. The one who taught me to swim when Mother wasn't looking. I reached out, tugged her by the arm. "Will you marry the Captain?"

She flushed and pulled away. "Don't think it's your place to ask."

The Captain's chuckle ran down his throat to somewhere near a growl. "Les, sometimes you have to know when to keep your cabin door shut. Tight."

Until I met the Captain I thought my first name was Boy. That's all Father called me. Not that he didn't say it pleasantly, as in, "For heaven's sake, Boy, don't let your mother know we've been up to Uncle Nolan's still."

If not for the Captain and big sisters Cal and Neva (what everyone called Nevada), I might never have heard my name spoken in childhood. My younger brother (by sixteen and a half months) was called Gus, short for August. He was born in May; maybe they were hoping for a girl.

Two bends beyond Deadman's Curve and Railroad Gulch the river narrowed to a stream. A mile farther east, alders and willows grew where the stream became no more than a babbling creek, easy to ford. That was our name, Ford; Miller Ford, my father's name. Miller had been the surname of one of his grandmothers.

Father once said you could always tell a man's roots in the old country. Cooper or Baker or Smith had been the family occupation when a name took hold and stuck. A blueblood didn't work a mill. A Ford once probably lived near the crossing of a stream or maybe it was a corruption of forge.

"How do you corrupt a word?" I asked the Captain the next time he stopped into the Guest House. I had the Fair sisters near cleaned out of their penny purses with poker, this new game Uncle Nolan showed me.

I clutched four aces close to my chest when I turned to listen to the Captain's response. He heeled his boots clean on the mat by the door. "The same way you corrupt a man," he said. "Let him think he's more than he really is. Then watch him run."

"Run?" I asked.

"Run away with your money or run away from the chance to earn it with an honest day's labor."

"Captain, you runnin' away from marryin' Cal?" With all eyes on the Captain, I slinked my fifth ace under my seat.

Most of the logging camps along the river had no names, just numbers that grew as the chopping moved inland. Names were reserved for significant places like Railroad Gulch, the Forks, or Clearwater Creek.

The family who ran the cookhouse at the Forks lost a baby son to diphtheria in the late winter after I turned five. They nailed shut a clear pine box, set it on an open flat car, and tied the coffin down. Where the straps broke and the coffin tumbled off into the brush was Deadboy Siding from then on.

Assuming the body had ridden the rails to the undertaker, the dead boy's family hitched two rigs to ride around to the mill town for the burial. Miles Standish himself, cranked upriver on a handcar to retrieve the body; Miles Standish, the company owner, the eighth Miles Standish in a direct line of Miles Standishes going straight back to the Mayflower.

Of course, he spoke several words at the service. Only phrase I recalled was "angel of death." While the circuit preacher droned I asked Ma, "Is Death real?"

"Yes, indeed," she whispered. "And he might just come after a little boy who doesn't pay his respects." She pressed a forefinger to her lips.

Brother Louis played the bugle at the funeral. Everyone in the family played. Father fiddled at dances down at the company hall, above the harbor. I'd sit on the edge of the stage while the toe of his right boot tapped out a tune; remember the smile on his face when I first learnt to slap the spoons in rhythm.

Mother knew how to draw the bow, too, but I recall her then as the church organist. Brothers and sisters picked up fiddles, banjos, and mandolins as easily as they learned to ride.

Morrie and Orrie rode horses since they were three, but there along the river one day I watched 'em clamber onto some docile steers; one after the other threw 'em in the grass. I looked on from the top rail of a fence. A Hereford bull, eating at the clover, moseyed over 'til he was right alongside. Mouth and drippy nose in the grass, he lingered there so long I couldn't resist. Slid down astride his back; him so wide my toes barely reached his flanks. He didn't seem to notice and carried me along to a new spot to munch. I patted his hide, his tail swatted me and a fly.

Leaned forward, grabbed his horns with both hands, and gave him a kick. He jerked and I flew, tumbling through sky, green grass spinning around me; landed on my bee-hind, like a whole hive stung me.

Rolled to my feet then marched right up to his white face. "You don't look like no Mr. Death. I won't take that, Mr. Bull." I socked him on his curly forehead.

He looked up, eyes reddened, hooves pawing at his turf, and the next thing I knew Morrie swung me by my waist way up in the air, not settin' me down 'til we're both far away from there.

That's how I got my start punching cattle.

At dinner that night Orrie told what happened. Ma frowned at me. "If you want to go riding bulls and broncs, that's fine, but if you break your neck, don't come crying home to me." ❖

"November Surf in Mendocino," Janet Ashford

The Next Coming

by Jewels Marcus

I'm not who you think I am.
Days of lush lazy lawns pregnant
with carefree laughing children
are long gone.
I'm your daughter's daughter.
The new messiah.
The coroner.
The next coming.
I'm walking on the backs of discarded plastic bottles,
across seas, in search of salvation and clean drinking water.
I'm sifting through un-majestic purple mountains of trash,
for the tainted treasure of tasteless scraps
to fill my aching empty guts.
I'm roaming radiated deserts for evidence of my inheritance.
I'm your judge   your jury   your coroner
stuffing the giant cracks you left in the scorched earth
with the putrid, swollen bodies of my kin.
I'm your daughter's daughter
needing to grow new lungs to filter the filthy air
new hands to claw over continents of blackened concrete.
I'm the one left after the last holocaust.
The one you didn't want to notice, too busy
entertaining yourselves   for one-third of your lives.

I'm not who you think I am.
I'm the minister   the preacher   the teacher.
My hopes and prayers like wolves sent out to devour our fears.
I'm the new messiah.   Walking on water.
The coroner.   Burying your future.
The next coming.

Non-Fiction

War Babies

by Willow Arthur

MY PARENTS FORM a discordant orchestra in the background of my life, never quite disappearing, sometimes elbowing their way forward to hog the limelight. Most people exist in drab tones of beige—not they. Until I grew up, I thought that everyone lived with their fever-pitch intensity, indulging in scenes of MacBethian drama.

When Mum and Dad find out about my memoir, they do not retreat into demure silence, fearful of the horrors that might leak out. Instead, they see it as an opportunity to shove everyone off the stage and emote.

On my last visit home to Colorado, my mother produces sumptuous meals for three days, accompanied by sparkling smiles, until a familiar thundercloud descends. A brooding hatches behind her expressionless blue eyes and furrowed brow. Wrapped in cold silence, she chops carrots, with fingers carefully separated by blood-splotched Band-Aids. Mum shoots furious glances at anyone who invades her kitchen. She is surrounded by innumerable cups of tepid English tea, which will prop her up in the dark hours to come. Her mood indicates she is exhausted and yet determined to pursue her culinary martyrdom to the bitter end. She will cook until she is discovered dead, drooped over the stove, her fingers sliced to ribbons.

It pays not to underestimate her. This is a woman who, after half a century, popped out a ten-pound baby. On 20 cups of tea a day. This is a woman who can read minds and wriggle your worst secret out before you know what's happening. Once, my ex-husband lost his job and we swore to keep it a secret so we wouldn't spoil Christmas.

Mum opened the front door and the warm air was fragrant with mince pies. "So, how *did* you lose your job?" said she.

The kitchen is declared a war zone. Like a bird of prey, Mum watches me and oldest brother John slink away. Her eyes harden into slits of suspicion. She has never forgotten we raided her food cupboard when we were ten years old, starving and rationed to two oily fish fingers plus peas a day. Cooked by a demented housekeeper who drooled and was even more frightening than Mum. So we stole from my parents' cupboard and stuffed ourselves with all the great food they'd stashed away for themselves.

Now we know to retreat. Before the yelling and the flying saucepans commence. Family members flee to the garden for self-preservation. Over potted chrysanthemums, we recall the time Mum threw John, her eldest son, out of the kitchen window because he annoyed her while she was cooking, then hurled my boots at me for leaving them on the kitchen floor. Luckily, I ducked, and Mum's ability to break windows before dinner became legendary.

My parents are thorough, not like my grandparents, who discreetly excused themselves and died with little fuss as soon as their duties were discharged. Mum and Dad will be parenting from their deathbeds, propped on their Swiss silk pillows and demanding attention.

Stretched out on lawn furniture, my brothers and I mournfully tally the number of our in-laws forced into alcoholism around the fringes of my mother's madness. My middle brother, slick and wealthy, teases my baby brother, whose conception was a miracle the year Mum turned fifty.

"One last bloody egg—and there he is," says James, the blond mogul, who is secretly the boss of the family now, much to Dad's furious resentment. Baby Flukey grins back, shirtless and remorseless, his red hair shooting out in a flaming halo. Mum's last egg is worshipped. He can do no wrong. Flukey meanders through college and no one cares if he never leaves home and never wins another tennis match.

James whispers to me that Mum and Dad rush eagerly to watch Flukey's tennis matches, and totter off home vaguely, like demented pensioners, when it's James' turn to play. My middle brother is trying to comfort me, pointing out I am not the only child singled out for their peculiar English nastiness.

Out on the lawn Dad grumbles to himself, stomping around with the dogs, trying to force a wee-wee out of them. "As soon as Luke gets out of college, that's it. I'm leaving your mother for good."

"Oh, rubbish Dad, nobody else will put up with you. Besides you'll be dead soon, what's the point?"

Dad heaves a weighty breath. Nobody comprehends his suffering. He fidgets and fusses over the dogs. He has acquired a huge German shepherd, who is completely untrainable and may have gobbled up a couple of grandchildren on the sly. Watching Dad, a memory bell sounds and I am transported to a moment thirty years earlier.

I stand in our stained London kitchen with its cracked linoleum and air of depressed functionality.

"Yup, as soon as you kids grow up. I'm launching my catamaran and sailing off around the world," Dad announces with finality. We feel a thrill of fear and Dad gazes out of the window, saying a silent goodbye to the soggy daffodils nodding in the rain.

I see endless vistas of gently rolling waves and anticipate a lot of minced-meat on toast, which is Dad's solitary accomplishment in the kitchen. I will be hungry but peaceful. I will only have to deal with Dad's dangerous conviction that he is the shark-killing ship's captain from *Jaws*.

"Can I come?" I say, sensing my betrayal, but also liberation from the endless to-do lists and detailed instructions Mum pins on every available wall-space in the house. Above the telephone bristles an admonition to spend no longer than two minutes talking. She tapes a caution on the bathroom mirror, to spend at least ten minutes brushing one's teeth. In the living room crouches a computer, like a monstrous, dusty spider, sprouting notes from Mum about the brain disorders it creates. For her, computers are enemy number one because they are Dad's greatest love.

Breaking Mum's rules is Dad's mission. He inveigles our support, which feels naughty, but we are too weak to resist. It takes a whole new generation before my Dad gets busted by my daughter. Firmly, she tells him to discuss his marital problems with Grandma and to quit bothering everyone else.

Over the decades, Mum takes Dad's betrayals stoically. She tightens her ship and narrows his options. When Dad is semi-delirious from back surgery, she confiscates his car keys and he thrashes around the house like a frenzied animal she's captured from the wild.

He thunders. "That woman will be the death of me. I've been imprisoned."

Mum is in deep trouble when she gets demoted from "your mother" to "that woman." Mum fancies Dad will crash in a ditch if he escapes, and under house arrest, dark moods overpower him. Dad has been known to snooze blissfully through red lights, so her concerns are not wildly misplaced. He talks his way out of innumerable car violations by pretending, in his most supercilious English accent, to have just got off the plane from England.

To spice things up, my father forces each of his children to promise to shoot him dead before he becomes a helpless, car-less invalid under Mum's supervision. Last summer he insisted on bringing his gun on holiday in the RV, in case the dirty deed needed doing.

Pathetically, he begs for medical marijuana to be smuggled in. "I'm fading away," Dad moans from the depths of his armchair, when he fails to locate any of his car keys.

"Nonsense," Mum retorts. She is proud that she eradicated the word "obey" in her marriage vows. It was her feminist gesture to the sixties, the decade of their courtship. But Mum and Dad never really made it into the sixties, and remain embalmed in the fifties.

Mum worked as a young make-up artist at the BBC when the Beatles made their first famous appearance. Slapping pancake on their baby faces and spraying their pudding-bowl haircuts, she became frightened. Mum and Dad dismissed the Beatles as crude, rude and vulgar. Those were my parents' final words on the Summer of Love. In contrast, I was a born flower child, lured to earth by the generation that refused to go to war and sang peace songs with petals falling from their hair. I never figured out why those colorful dreams faded and hippies were usurped by yuppies in Thatcher's gray London of my childhood.

But the war babies, born too early to adjust to LSD and free love, are tougher than old alligator skins. My parents won't go gently into the night. Mum was born while the bombs were dropping on England and we speculate that her brain never recovered from the shock. Her abandonment fears seem extreme and, to keep them at bay, she places Dad on a strict no sugar, no cholesterol regime. His creamy black tea disappears and, instead, he swirls green tea suspiciously. His four spoonfuls of white sugar are replaced with life-giving agave nectar.

"I'll keep you alive forever. What on earth would I do without you?" Mum says.

Dad's suffering at Mum's hands has been corroborated by hard medical evidence. My father is a doctor's son and believes in documenting his physical and emotional distress for the benefit of future generations. He loves to tell the tale of how, during their seven-year engagement, he went to see a "nerve specialist" about a terribly upset stomach. The doctor requested an interview with Dad's fiancée to get a full diagnostic picture. According to Dad, the specialist spent a few minutes alone with Mum and took Dad aside, whispering. "To survive this marriage, you will need to take six anti-anxiety pills a day for the rest of your life. My God, good luck, old man."

Dad laughs uproariously at this point in his tale and a small, rueful smile curls around the corners of Mum's mouth. They are so fond of their dark comedy, it is impossible to extrapolate the truth.

"Back then, your father needed two confidence pills to get out of bed in the morning," Mum retaliates. "Prescribed by *his* father, Dr. Arthur. He was a walking medical encyclopedia, hooked on every imaginable psychiatric drug. He had migraine headaches and boils oozing down his neck. That was before I took over," she states firmly.

"It was the stress of dealing with your family," Dad says. "None of whom came to the wedding, thank God. All mad as hat-stands, fading aristocracy, living on tin mines with no tin in them. Inbred stock you know, no business acumen left. All waffle, fancy Knightsbridge addresses and no dough."

Mum refuses to give up her innumerable relatives, the ones who don't blur reality with booze and are dumb enough to pick fights with Dad. He exiled a good portion of the family tree for crimes against his dignity. Mum visits hospitals, holds their dying hands and makes clucking sounds of commiseration when they mention my father's temper.

"Your brother Geoffrey came over and pinched my gun off the wall. Claimed it was his," roars Dad.

"Well, it was!" Mum points out. "It was his inheritance."

"He robbed you of every penny that was due."

Dad rounds on his children, who are riveted, as usual, by our parents' horribleness. It is better than *Dynasty*. "Your poor mother grew desperate for me before our engagement. Told me awful lies. Said she needed someone to look after all her money and imaginary tin mines. When that failed, she took up residence on the Royal Albert Bridge and threatened to jump off unless I married her within the year."

My parents are most happy when fate throws them a natural disaster to unite them in love against the forces of evil. Forest fires are their favorite form of entertainment and regress them to the two resourceful children who once survived the bombs of WWII.

In the hot, dry Colorado summer, flames frequently threaten to engulf their mountain home and they enjoy scoffing when the Sheriff's department calls with evacuation orders. Dad thinks the cops are lacking in true grit. Sometimes my elder brother John phones, pretending to be the Sheriff's department. "To give them something to live for," he says. "Stimulates their nerve-endings."

Exactly what Dad used to say, 30 years earlier, when he abandoned us in the English woods at twilight.

"Bugger off," Dad yells down the telephone to the real or imaginary Sheriff. "Mandatory means maximum allowable force. We will never surrender. Not in a million years. You will have to cart us out in coffins." Dad is proud of the fact that he Googled the word "mandatory" and reclaimed his right to cook himself in his own house.

He flounders about looking for the cracks in the walls where he hid his gold coins. He herds Mum and the three dogs down into the basement where they crouch amongst rations of canned food until the last fire-engines screech by to set up road-blocks. When it is safe to emerge, Mum and Dad crawl up on the roof clutching thermoses of hot chocolate. They station themselves on the coarse shingles, armed with hoses to wet down their property. They will force away the fire licking the perimeter of their precious home. Mum and Dad were evacuated at five years old and will never be evacuated again.

Sitting on the roof, keeping the flames at bay, they are happier than two children swinging their legs over a river. They are a pair of kids who have managed to miss the last school bus home. ❖

FICTION

On the Thursday Before Easter

AN EXCERPT FROM THE NOVEL *OLD TESTAMENT EYES*

BY NORMA WATKINS

GOING CRAZY FEELS LIKE BEES in my head. Crazy isn't a term I would choose, but I heard my sister Wingate whisper, "She's crazy" to Aunt Pat last Christmas. Now I can't get it out of my head. Trust my older sister to say something hateful. Crazy is a word like nigger and nobody should be allowed to use it who doesn't participate in the condition. I prefer calling these *the bad times*: the days when my nerves fray, I can't hear for the buzzing, and feel myself climbing toward a fall.

On this, the Thursday before Easter, the pressure is building. I didn't sleep—again—laid in the dark with my legs jerking like a dog's until I gave up, crept out of the room without waking Walton and came downstairs. Drank an entire pot of Union Coffee with chicory. Now it's seven in the morning with the sun coming in like a shotgun blast through the window over the sink. Squinting, I rinse the empty pot and start a new one. When I can't sleep and quit eating, when the buzz in my head gets me moving double time, a crash is on the way. Once I tried romanticizing it, telling myself I was cycling in harmony with the earth and turning away from the dark. A lot of blah-blah.

Talking to Dr. McNair, my psychiatrist, I blame my husband Walton or my daughter Margaret, the beloved family unit. Nothing in this house ever goes the way it's supposed to, especially holidays. The fight to get everything done ratchets me up. I'm tap-dancing on the walls to keep them happy, clacking across the ceiling to preserve peace, dancing so fast I defy gravity. Until the crash. The doctor says my mania is caused by a chemical imbalance, and to stop blaming circumstances. But Christmas and Easter are also the times when my sister Wingate returns—the darling, prodigal daughter, everybody's favorite. I need to be crazy to face her.

I hear Walton on the stairs. Even his feet sound neat, with exactly the same pace and pressure on each tread. He comes into the kitchen and I smile, pretending to have awakened early instead of not sleeping. After 26 years, he knows me and I have no intention of going to the hospital yet. I will not give Wingate the satisfaction of visiting the psychiatric ward this year. "I've made coffee."

He is armored for his day, the crisp shirt tucked in back with two precise pleats, the gray trousers creased, twin ceiling lights reflecting off his polished shoes. He pours a cup, unfolds the paper and sits down.

I drum my fingers on the tabletop in a checkerboard of sunlight.

"Please don't do that."

I stop. "Would you like some fresh-squeezed orange juice?"

"No, thanks." He doesn't look at me and it's just as well. I have on the APG, the All Purpose Garment he despises, a green sack with yellow stripes, my favorite outfit because it zips up the front and I can step into it and be dressed in two seconds. I haven't combed my hair or put on lipstick. My mother Big Win—may she rest in peace—said a lady should always greet her husband perfectly put together, makeup on and hair in place. I haven't passed by a mirror, but I suspect after a night awake, my face looks like a bowl of tapioca.

"How about half a grapefruit?"

"Not today."

"Toast?" I'm taunting him now, waiting for that little twitch of annoyance and I get it.

"I'd like to be left alone to read the paper if I may."

Hanford has a dreadful paper, too insipid to read. I prefer *The New York Times*, but they have to drive it down from Memphis, and it doesn't get to town until afternoon. Walton claims it's too expensive anyway.

"Could you turn that radio off?"

I push the button. Listening to Public Radio connects me, at least temporarily, to the world outside. Walton can't stand hearing noise while he reads. I look at his nose, pointing into the fold of the paper, eyes darting down a column. This is my husband, the man I will be with until death does us part. I press a hand against my chest. You shouldn't have thoughts that make you want to be dead. On the back of the newspaper is a full-page ad for the Valley Gas Company, the woman in the picture smiling down on her new gas grill. If we had a thing like that, Walton could barbecue and I'd only have to make salads.

"What do you think about a gas grill?"

He puts the paper down with a rattle. "A what?"

I point to the ad. "A grill." My hand shakes. "To cook out on."

"We have a grill." He means the rusty hibachi on the brick patio.

"But not a—"

"Are you going to let me read this paper?"

"Read, read." I get up and pour myself another cup of coffee, my ninth, or twelfth. I slide in my bedroom slippers around the kitchen, singing. "Blue Moon, I saw you standing alone ..." I can never remember more than the first line of songs. "I loved those Saturday nights when we were first married and we used to go dancing at the country club."

"That was your parents, not us."

I stop, left foot on a white linoleum square, right on a black. "Are you sure? Can you misappropriate a memory?"

Walton folds the paper with a snap. "Are you happy? You've succeeded in driving me out of my own house." He takes his suit jacket off the back of the chair, puts it on, adjusts the lapels and buttons one button. He tucks the folded paper under his arm, exactly the way he does every morning, except some days I don't drive him away and he leaves the paper for me. I would enjoy reading the funnies and the obituaries, which face one another in the Women's Section, but I don't ask. Being left with no paper is my punishment for irritating him. Look at the man, like an ad for the successful, middle-aged Republican: body fit, hair short, skin pink, and conscience clear. "Bye, darling." I tilt a cheek for a kiss. He pecks. "Have a wonderful day." I say it like a good wife and then ruin things by cackling.

"God, Tyler."

I wave until he rounds the corner of the house. At the car, he will remove the jacket and hang it on a hook above the rear window. More than anything in the world, Walton craves a Ferrari. If he could trade me in for one, I'd be trussed like a pig this minute and on my way out the door. He drives a dark blue BMW, the sporty model, but he longs for a red Ferrari. "Hangar queens," I say whenever he mentions this wish. That's what they call cars that need a lot of repairs. I like watching him flush, swallowing the anger, Adam's apple going up and down.

I pour the last cup of coffee down the sink and fill a glass with tap water. I will drink eight of these and flush this breakdown away. Not a good sign, starting the day with Walton angry and me feeling mean as a snake.

Why did we get married in the first place? He was my first boyfriend and the qualities that drive me insane now were the attraction. He was quiet and competent; he wasn't a greaser. You could see from the way he wore his clothes he wouldn't let the bills go unpaid. I liked how he ducked his head and chuckled when I said something funny. Not that he does that anymore. Neither one of us have uttered an amusing word in years.

I didn't realize back then that Walton's silence went all the way to the bone—the man doesn't talk. Moderation is his rule, which means he seldom gets raging mad, but almost never shows any real joy either. Dr. McNair says I'm lucky, not many men can live with mental illness. I tell her men *cause* mental illness, which makes her smile the way psychiatrists do when they think you're nutty, but don't want to lose your business. Walton hasn't left me, I'll give him that, but he gets a little too much grim-lipped pleasure out of signing me into the hospital after one of my crashes. He is the long-suffering husband and I get to be the cracked wife, which is not the way I planned it.

Night. I made it through the day without breaking—holding myself together like a cracked egg. Went shopping with Margaret and bought us both Easter outfits, in spite of a terrible row over what was appropriate, involving flung clothes and Margaret stomping out of the store. Paid a weekly visit to Miss Pat, sipping tea from one of my aunt's dirty cups, my hands shaking like a spastic, managing to swallow the stale pound cake without choking. Fixed a dinner of dry pork chops and canned green beans, a dinner Margaret wouldn't come out of her room for and Walton only picked at.

An idea comes while I'm running hot water over the dirty plates. If I make it through the next three days, manage to get past Easter lunch with my father, and Wingate's visit, I'll give myself a present. Drive to Ocean Springs, walk on the wet sand and let the salt water lap at my feet until my head gets quiet. I'm not sure where I'll find the money for such a trip, but that is a problem for later.

Every day ends the same—back in bed with Walton. Going to bed with my nerves twanging like banjo strings is like prison, night being the sentence, morning the parole.

Walton locks himself in the hall bathroom for two hours every night. I know most of his routine from the noise or lack of it: a long sit on the toilet, a longer bath, and a shower to wash off the bath water. I suspect masturbation, except I can't imagine Walton doing anything so messy. Where would he do it—under the shower, maybe, or sitting on the toilet, surely not in his bath water. I try to imagine his fantasies—the naughty nurse? The naughty Ferrari salesgirl? Certainly not me.

Walton comes in with his blue pajamas buttoned to the top, carrying a mystery novel.

I pull the robe closer around my neck and shift my legs away as he gets in bed.

He says, "Are you sleeping in your robe?"

"I'm cold."

"I can get another blanket."

Always polite, so civil. We could be strangers on a train, forced to share adjoining seats for the night, except the nights will go on until I die, and during every one of them I will lie beside this particular stranger.

Walton settles on his pillows and opens his book. "Did you take your medication?"

"Ummm." I close my eyes, fold my hands over my chest and try to look asleep.

"Does that noise mean yes?"

"Ummm."

"I'm asking for your own good. If you don't take your medication, you'll end up in the hospital again. You and I both know that."

"Ummm." This is getting to be fun.

"Shall I go in the bathroom and count the pills?"

I'm in the kind of prison where the warden comes into the cell, climbs into your bunk, and spends the night interrogating you. I sit up suddenly enough to make Walton flinch, and there is the small pleasure of that, the ability after all these years to make your husband jump, the private knowledge that, in spite of his armor, I make him afraid.

"I took the fucking pill, okay? Now can I sleep?"

"Please don't use that language, Tyler."

"Fuck, fuck, fuck."

"It's really unattractive coming out of a woman's mouth."

"Fuck, shit… fuck." I can't think of any more words. I need a whole new vocabulary of colorful curses.

"You're trying to aggravate me."

"Read your book."

We lie side by side. I long to take my head in my hands to quiet the buzzing, but not in front of Walton. "What are you doing all that time in the bathroom, playing with yourself?" I feel him stiffen.

"I won't do this, Tyler."

I mock him. "I won't do this, Tyler."

"Why do you wait until bedtime to start a quarrel?"

"If you had half the brain you pretend to, you might remember that I didn't start this quarrel. I was lying here peacefully trying to sleep."

"You don't fool me. You stay in bed until you think I'm asleep and then you get up. You haven't slept for three nights."

"If you're not going to read, Walton, turn out the light."

"Have you been going out again?"

"Not in your car, darling. I wouldn't dare."

"It's dangerous, Tyler, driving around at night in your state."

"The State of Confusion, I presume? The State of Insanity?"

"You know what I mean."

"Walton, I'm not in the car. I'm right here beside you and I've taken my pill. Could you please read, or turn off the light and be quiet?"

"You say we never talk."

"This isn't talk, it's an inquisition."

"I'm concerned. I ask these questions because I want to keep you safe."

"I'm locked in here safe for the night. Can we sleep, warden?"

"What did you call me?"

"Walton. I said Walton."

Three more days. I close my eyes and see the sand, feel the sun warming my head and the calm waters of the Gulf curling over my feet. I can do this. ❖

Non-Fiction

Anthracite

by Charles Furey

CATHY MORLEY'S THICK BLACK HAIR hangs down the back of her neck and her eyes are the color of violets. In our busy classroom she is always quiet and reserved, but when she jumps Double Dutch at recess, her laughter rings across the playground. In the five months I have been in this school, four desks behind hers in the fifth grade row, she has not smiled at me once. Her father is a coal dealer. He keeps the different kinds of coal in wooden bins in the yard beside his house.

Gray smoke rises from the chimney as I approach their place this bitter cold morning. In the only secure pocket of my corduroys I have seven crumpled dollar bills, a quarter, two dimes and a nickel. Mother placed it in my care as if it were a great treasure. It better still be there when I am ready to pay Mister Morley for a half ton of nut-sized anthracite coal.

Cathy is surprised to see me when she finds me waiting at her back door. Her hair is braided this morning. For the first time I notice the freckles dusting her nose. She does not smile in greeting. When I tell her the reason for my visit, she says, "Wipe the snow off your shoes and come in." These cold words are the first she has ever spoken to me and I pause for a moment to wonder at their beauty. "Come in," she says again, without yet using my name.

Mr. Morley, with his shirt sleeves rolled up, lounges at the breakfast table reading the morning paper. The china plate in front of him is smeared with egg yolk. He is chewing a piece of toast, sipping a cup of coffee. The Morley kitchen is snug and warm and I know, without any hope of ever visiting them, the other rooms are just as comfortable, the way all houses should be in wintertime. "What can I do for you, young man?" Mr. Morley wipes his mouth with a napkin.

"I want to buy some coal," I say. Mother has already found out that it costs fifteen dollars a ton.

"Fine," Mr. Morley says, and smiles encouragingly at me. "How much coal?"

"A half ton," I say.

His smile fades. "Do you have a truck? Do you have some way to pick it up here at the yard?"

He obviously does not mean that I, personally, have a truck. "No," I answer.

"I don't deliver less than a ton," he says, looking closely at me now, as if he is seeing me for the first time.

"We have a wagon," I say, "and a gunny sack, and me and my brother Joe can—"

"Dad!" Cathy draws out the sound of her father's name.

Mister Morley lays his newspaper aside and leans forward to study Cathy and me, standing side by side in front of him, placing me now in the same age group as his daughter, making the connection that we are possibly classmates. He has no way, however, of knowing the immense distance between us, more now than those four desks that separate us at school. But he is beginning to guess. "Well, all right then, where do you live?" He asks as if my answer will make all the difference in his decision.

"On Bellevue Avenue. The gray house next to the Acme Market, three blocks from here."

"Okay," he says after another long pause. "I'll deliver it sometime this afternoon."

"Thank you," I say, and hand him my fistful of warm coins and crumpled dollar bills.

When Cathy holds the storm door open for me, I thank her also, meaning thanks for persuading your father to help us. But I can tell by the expression in her eyes this briefest of associations is likely the last I will ever have with her.

The snow continues throughout the rest of the morning and is still drifting down in the late afternoon when Mister Morley backs his truck into our driveway. I run out to show him where to dump the coal. The truck-bed tilts and the coal clatters out. Then without saying "So long," without even acknowledging my mother watching from the kitchen window, he drives away.

Joe and I fetch shovels and buckets and start to lug the precious fuel into the house. This small pile will not last us very long. A half-ton of anthracite is not much to start with. A half-ton of coal spilled onto the ground in a foot of deepening snow is hardly any coal at all. ❖

Non-Fiction

Donald from the Hame

by Janet Ashford

Los Angeles, 1969

"Want to go to Long Beach and stay at my parents' house for a couple of days, John? They're going away and want me to keep an eye on my brother." I tried to sound casual, afraid he wouldn't want to do anything so ordinary, but it would be better if he came along.

I first noticed John at an orchestra rehearsal and asked my friend Jennie who he was. She said he had a girlfriend, but I wormed myself into his affections and he dumped her, saying it was almost over anyway. He was tall and skinny, with a reddish beard and thick blond hair that waved to his chin. His face was always flushed and his light blue eyes had puffy upper lids that made him look inscrutable. After we were together a few months, he gave me a ring, a worn amethyst in a filigree setting that had been cut off the finger of an aunt. Sometimes a bit of my skin got pinched in the gap of the band, so I tried to be careful.

John and I lived at West Adams Gardens—a group of 1920s Tudor revival buildings north of campus. The white plaster facades were outlined with wide dark boards and the large rooms had high ceilings and big, bright windows. Past their prime, the apartments were rundown and cheap, but still elegant. John's place was upstairs in the building by the street and mine in the next building back. I had a single bed, but John had a double, so I spent most of my nights with him. My parents didn't know this, and would not want me to have John at their place when they were gone, but my brother would never tell.

"Mom wants me to visit Grandma Florrie too," I said.

"Have I met her?"

"I don't think so. She's never been up here."

"What's she like?"

"She's pretty interesting. She's an artist."

John and I were having coffee alone in the dining room. During dinner, my roommate Jennie had told a story about Clark House, the old mansion the music school used for private lessons. The student who managed scheduling was having strange experiences there.

"Skip was alone last Friday getting ready to lock up," Jennie had said. "He was going away for the weekend so he'd brought his suitcase. He had to go upstairs to make sure the rooms were empty, but the front door was open for people to go out. He locked the door of the office with the suitcase inside. He checked everything, went back to the office, unlocked the door, and there was his suitcase still lying open, and his clothes thrown all over the room."

John knew Skip. "He told me. Freaky."

"Is Clark House haunted?" I'd asked.

"I've heard people say it is," Molly, my other roommate, had said. "Skip says he hears footsteps on the stairs when he's alone there at night."

"Wow." I wanted to believe in anything supernatural, though it scared me.

Molly and Jennie had gone to their rooms to practice and now John and I heard the clash of a Baroque oboe and a violin struggling with Khachaturian as we lingered at the table. I should have been practicing too, but used John as an excuse to delay. He got out his cigarettes, took one, and passed the rest to me. He smoked Winstons, so I did, too. They always made me think of my high school English teacher's complaint about their slogan, which should be "Winston tastes good *as* a cigarette should." It was an example of how commerce overruns culture.

I lit my ungrammatical cigarette. "Grandma Florrie's paintings are all over her house. I used to stare at them when I was a kid. She had a book called *The Lost Continent of Mu* and I always wondered what that was."

"Didn't you ask her?"

"No," I said, surprised. "I never thought of doing that. It was just there. It sounded mysterious."

"Like the ghost in Clark House?" he said and I laughed. "Sure, I'll go with you. We can watch the TV and raid your parents' kitchen. I wouldn't mind visiting your Grandma. I like old people if they're interesting. We can ask her about Mu."

That's how we came to be approaching Leisure World one gray Saturday afternoon, driving through a dispiriting flatland of oil refineries, small factories, and fields of dusty lettuce. Passing the entrance, I directed John through the many turns to Grandma's place, a two-bedroom unit in one of the endless rows of low ugly buildings.

"This is worse than where your parents live," John said as we got out of the car.

"I know, both places are awful." When I was sixteen, my parents sold the small but well-built house in Compton where I grew up and bought a sterile two-story tract house in Long Beach. I had to spend my last two years of high school among strangers. Grandma had been forced out of her home too. "Grandma and Grandpa had a nice little house at the beach. I loved going there when I was a kid."

"Why did she leave?"

"The relatives were afraid she couldn't live by herself after Grandpa died, though she's been doing fine for five years." I told John what happened. My grandfather died suddenly of a heart attack while he and Grandma stood in line to renew his driver's license. It had been a shock, and she was sad and discouraged for a while. But in time she regained her mild, cheerful manner. She lived in an apartment near her son, then moved to Leisure World when she needed more "help." Grandpa had been a quiet, gentle man, with thick white hair and a kindly face. I remembered her fussing to make him put on a sweater when it was chilly. They had been happy together.

We walked up and knocked on the front door. Grandma opened it quickly and I saw her familiar form. She was old and had been for the whole time I knew her. She married late at thirty-two and was sixty-three when I was born, so for me she was always an elderly person with a soft wrinkled face and a faintly sweet smell from the powder that caked in the cracks along her cheeks. She had filmy blue eyes almost hidden in the folds around them, but a finely-pointed, straight nose. Like most old ladies, she wore her pale gray hair in short curls, maintained by a weekly visit to the beauty parlor. She never wore pants, but dressed in stockings, low-heeled shoes, and shirtwaist dresses in small flowered prints like the one she was wearing now.

"It's little Janet. I haven't seen you for quite a time." She got me into a hug.

"This is my friend John," I said. "He's a musician. He plays the piano."

He put out his hand and Grandma smiled. "You'll have to speak up, John, I'm a bit hard of hearing."

"I'm glad to meet you," he said, in a slightly louder-than-normal voice. He looked toward the walls hung with Grandma's art. "Are these your paintings?"

John knew how to be polite to old people. I'd seen him do it at the Presbyterian church where he got paid to rehearse the choir. I went with him to sing for morning service and sometimes we were invited home by a choir member for Sunday dinner. Grandma was so pleased by John's attention that she gave him a tour of her work.

She led him from one to the next. There were the two large paintings that fascinated me as a child: one of a wagon train coming through a mountain pass and the other of a California mission. Both were on un-stretched canvas hanging from braided rope. Her smaller pieces, in ornate wooden frames, included seascapes, desert scenes, still life groupings, and sailboats on the ocean at sunset. The paintings were not bad, but not particularly good. Grandma had many "How to Paint" books and it seemed she did her best to follow their instructions.

"These are nice," said John, also doing his best.

I looked around. The apartment was clean and well fitted out, but so impersonal that even the paintings didn't make it a home. The living and dining areas were one large room, but there were windows on only one wall, so it felt dark and confined. The player piano from the beach house was gone, left in my uncle's garage where no one used it. The rest of Grandma's familiar things were there—even the bookcase that held *The Lost Continent of Mu*—but the old furniture looked out of place. The apartment was a space designed to accommodate a succession of old people who would deploy their knickknacks for a few years and then fade away.

There was another knock on the door and Grandma let in an old man in a black suit. "This is my brother Elmer," she said to John. "He and I are the only ones left. All the others have gone on ahead."

Uncle Elmer shook hands with John and we stood awkwardly until Grandma walked toward the kitchen counter.

"Come sit at the table," she said. "I'll get the lunch."

Uncle Elmer looked fragile and seemed older than Grandma, though he was seven years younger. He was bony and beak-nosed, with transparent skin, a few strands of white hair combed back from his forehead, and that odd smell old people sometimes have. When I was ten, he gave me hard-bound, children's editions of *Treasure Island* and *The Swiss Family Robinson* for Christmas, and years later a cousin said the grown-ups had grumbled because the books were used. But I treasured those volumes and still had them.

Elmer had lived with his sisters Emmie and Clara in an old house south of downtown, over-full of tables, chests, and worn upholstered chairs. Each old aunt said, "How big you are," and kissed my cheek with dry lips. I was surprised their skin that looked so wrinkled, felt soft against my face. Grandma was the fourth and Elmer the last of six children. Three had married and three had not, and I never learned why the singles ended up that way. Four had died and Grandma Florrie was now eighty-three and Elmer seventy-six. John and I would never be that old.

"Florence says you are a music student at USC, along with Janet," Elmer said as we sat.

"Yes sir, that's where we met," said John.

"I hear it's quite a good school."

"It's considered the best on the west coast."

"Is that so?"

Grandma put a plate of sandwiches on the table. "There's baloney and cheese and peanut butter and jelly. Take your pick." The cheese was Swiss, with lettuce and bright yellow mustard; the jelly was grape. Both were on soft white bread. Grandma opened a bag of potato chips. There was a bowl with apples, oranges and bananas—the standard fruits—and a small dish of crinkle cut sweet pickles. I took one of each kind of sandwich. We ate and chatted across the generations.

"I see you're letting your hair grow," said Grandma. My dark hair, parted in the middle, reached the tops of my shoulders.

"John told me he'd like it better long than short," I said.

Grandma and her brother looked at John with approval. Then she said, "Did I ever tell you Janet, about how your grandfather and I were married?"

"No, how did it happen?" As with Mu, I'd never thought about it. They were just always together.

"I was working in the city back then. I rode up to New York on the train from Plainfield, where we all lived in the big house. It was a long ride and I was tired when I got home. But one evening as I came in, Emmie ran up and said, 'Florrie, someone wants to talk to us. I think there's a message for you.' So we got Clara and went upstairs to the Ouija board."

"What's a Ouija board?" I asked.

Uncle Elmer leaned back and put his hands behind his head. John leaned forward.

"It's a board with letters and numbers and the words *yes* and *no*," said John. "Right, Mrs. Munro?" Grandma nodded.

"We had a special one our father made. We called it The Chart. We had seen a Ouija board at a friend's house and the first time my mother used it, she got a clear message from her father who died at sea before she was born. So Daddy made us our own chart and Clara used it mainly. She and mother were natural mediums. Clara didn't use the pointer. She closed her eyes and moved her fingers around the chart while Emmie wrote down what letters she touched. After the first few words, Clara spoke out whole sentences. She was the most sensitive. She's the one who received *The Verses*."

"*The Verses*?" I asked.

"Clara got them in 1912, from our brother Willy who died when he was two. They told of the murder of Archduke Ferdinand that started World War One. So when Ferdinand *was* assassinated in 1914, we were pretty shook up."

John and I looked at each other. This was better than the ghost at Clark House.

"What happened to *The Verses*?" I asked.

"I have them still. Would you like a copy? They have copy machines here at Leisure World. Anyway, Emmie and Clara and I went up to the third floor where we could be quiet. There were a lot of us living in the house then—my mother and dad, my brother Walter and his wife Hazel and their children, as well as our sister Bertie and Elmer here."

"It must have been a big house," said John.

"It had three floors and people didn't mind sharing in those days," said Grandma. "Clara put her fingers on the chart and Emmie wrote down the words she spoke. She wrote: 'What would ye think, me fair lassies, if I wrote ye a letter from the Hame?' and signed it 'Donald Munro.'

"'Why that's Jim's father's name,' I said to Emmie, and the spirit said, 'Yes, I am Jim's father.' You see, your grandfather and I had been engaged, but we quarreled and I had not seen him for five years. I was the one who broke the engagement, and I was too proud to say I was sorry. I went to work as a commercial artist in New York, and I met people and didn't want to settle down anyway."

John looked at me and raised an eyebrow.

"Jim's father Donald came over from Scotland with his wife and the older children. You know *hame* is what they call *home* over there. Jim was born in New York, but his father died and three years later their mother died, and Jim was sent back to Edinburgh when he was only ten years old. He went to his Aunt Dolly Gordon, one of his mother's sisters, and she was good to him. Dolly's daughter Nellie was like his own sister and he never forgot them. That's why your mother's middle name is Gordon, after Aunt Dolly."

"I didn't know that," I said. "Mom doesn't like Gordon because it's a man's name."

"I don't know why Alice is so silly," said Grandma. "She knows who she's named for. Anyway, I said to the spirit, 'I guess Jim's married by now,' but Donald said, "No."

"'Then perhaps he's in the service. I haven't heard from him.' It was 1918 when this happened.

"'No,' said Donald, 'he is not in the service. You were destined for each other. I want you to get in touch with him.'

"I was struck by this, but I wanted to make sure. 'How do I know you're really Jim's father?' I asked the spirit. 'You'll have to prove it after all this time.'

"Donald said, 'There's been a baby born in this house and that child will be named after me and that's how you'll know.'"

"Was there a baby?" asked John, all attention.

"Yes. Hazel, Walter's wife, had given birth two days before and we knew she hadn't picked a name. We went right to her room where she was sitting in bed with the infant. Her boy Richard was there, home from school. He was only six years old. We rushed in and I asked, 'Hazel, have you picked a name for that baby?'

"She said no, she hadn't. 'I think I'll let his big brother name him. Richard dear, what would you like to call our new baby?'

"Richard was shy. He thought about it. 'There's a nice boy who sits next to me at school, and his name is Donald.'

"Well, that was it. To say we were dumbfounded is putting it mildly," said Grandma. John and I were dumbfounded too, sitting with eyebrows raised high. Uncle Elmer continued to lean back and look pleased. "We told Hazel that Donald was a good name and left the room. 'Now I'll have to try to find Jim. I'm so upset, Emmie.'

"We went downstairs to the telephone. I didn't know where Jimmy was, but I knew his older brother Alex. He and his wife lived a few streets over. I found the number and called them. 'Alex, I've had a message from your father. He says to get in touch with Jimmy right away. Do you know where he is?'

"'He's right here in the living room,' said Alex. 'I'll put him on.' I felt weak. I heard Jimmy's voice saying hello and it sounded so familiar." I saw that Grandma's thin gold wedding band was still on her left hand and I touched the ring on my finger.

"'Jim, this is Florrie. We've had a message from your father from the hame, and he told me to contact you.' I could tell by his voice that he was shaky too.

"'I'll be right over,' he said. There was a small woods near our house and we went there together to talk. We decided that if his father could see us so plainly, we would stay together. We were married three days later."

"Three days!" said John and I together.

"Well," she said, looking surprised, "it took some time to get the license." ❖

ACKNOWLEDGEMENTS

We want to thank the members who submitted pieces and everyone who worked to make this first volume a reality.

• Our officers: Doug Fortier, President, Malcolm Macdonald, Vice-President, Amie McGee, Treasurer, and Ginny Rorby, Secretary.

• Editor Norma Watkins for coordinating the judging, revisions and proof-reading.

• The judges: Henrietta Bensussen, Katherine Brown, Maureen Eppstein, Patty Joslyn, Malcolm MacDonald, Barbara MacKay, Amie McGee, Ginny Rorby, and Norma Watkins.

• Our careful proof-readers, Alena Deerwater, Patty Joslyn, Jewels Marcus, Fran Schwartz, Nona Smith, and Holly Tannen.

• The layout and design artist, Janet Ashford, our cover designer, Doug Fortier, and contributing artist and photographers: Alena Guest, Patty Joslyn, and Janet Ashford.

• We would like to especially thank Cynthia Frank of Cypress House for her help in guiding us through the process.